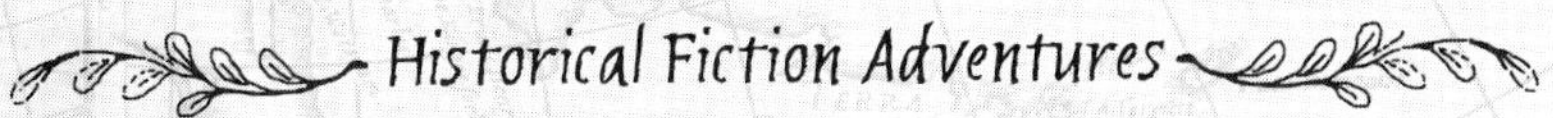

Pirate Hannah Pritchard

Captured!

Bonnie Pryor

Enslow Publishers, Inc.
40 Industrial Road
Box 398
Berkeley Heights, NJ 07922
USA
http://www.enslow.com

To Aaron, our newest little rebel

This book is a work of fiction. References to real people, events, establishments, organizations, or locales are intended only to provide a sense of authenticity, and are used to advance the fictional narrative. All other characters, and all incidents and dialogue, are drawn from the author's imagination and are not to be construed as real.

Library of Congress Cataloging-in-Publication Data:

Pryor, Bonnie.
Pirate Hannah Pritchard : captured! / Bonnie Pryor.
p. cm. — (Historical fiction adventures (HFA))
Includes bibliographical references (p.)
Summary: After seizing control of a British war ship, Hannah Pritchard, masquerading as a boy, and her pirate crewmates discover treasure, but are captured and imprisoned by British soldiers and endure torture and sickness before escaping.
ISBN-13: 978-0-7660-3310-8
ISBN-10: 0-7660-3310-4
[1. Pirates—Fiction. 2. United States—History—Revolution, 1775-1783—Fiction. 3. Survival—Fiction. 4. Sex role—Fiction.] I. Title.
PZ7.P94965Pi 2009
[Fic]—dc22

2008038629

This is a work of juvenile fiction.

Printed in the United States of America

10 9 8 7 6 5 4 3 2 1

To Our Readers: We have done our best to make sure all Internet Addresses in this book were active and appropriate when we went to press. However, the author and the publisher have no control over and assume no liability for the material available on those Internet sites or on other Web sites they may link to. Any comments or suggestions can be sent by e-mail to comments@enslow.com or to the address on the back cover.

Enslow Publishers, Inc., is committed to printing our books on recycled paper. The paper in every book contains 10% to 30% post-consumer waste (PCW). The cover board on the outside of each book contains 100% PCW. Our goal is to do our part to help young people and the environment too!

Illustration Credits: *The American Revolution: A Picture Source Book*, Dover Publications, Inc., 1975, p. 155; Library of Congress, pp. 156, 157, 158; Original Painting by © Corey Wolfe, p. 1

Cover Illustration: Original Painting by © Corey Wolfe.

Contents

The Story So Far . . .

The following is a brief account of the adventures Hannah Pritchard had before the tale you are about to read. Should you like to know in detail about all the close calls Hannah had and the battles she fought, check out Hannah Pritchard: Pirate of the Revolution *by Bonnie Pryor.*

The year is 1777 and the American colonies are fighting for their independence in the Revolutionary War. Fourteen-year-old Hannah Pritchard has returned to her farm to find her mother, father, and brother, Jack, murdered by a raiding party made up of the Iroquois, British, and Tories. Vowing revenge, she makes her way to Portsmouth, New Hampshire.

Learning that there is a privateer ship ready to plunder treasure from British merchant ships, Hannah makes a bold move. She disguises herself as a boy named Jack so that she can serve under the imposing Captain Nelson and get her revenge on the British. Life at sea is much harder than Hannah thought it to be, but she remains strong and learns the ins and outs of being a cabin boy. She meets Daniel, another sailor, and finds another friend in the gruff ship's cook, Dobbs.

However, a sailor named Larson constantly harasses and sets traps for Hannah. Plus the hated British are patrolling the seas, hoping to blow American privateers out of the water. Larson tries to frame Hannah, but is thwarted by the quick thinking of her friends. Hannah and her fellow sailors then try to capture a British ship. It is only through Hannah's bravery and cleverness that they defeat the British and sail away with the captured ship.

Now, in the year 1779, Hannah and her friends have to navigate treacherous waters infested with British frigates if they are to get back to Portsmouth. What dangers lurk ahead? Will they make it home safe? Read on to find out.

chapter one

Aboard the *Majestic*

High above the deck of the captured British ship the *Majestic*, Hannah Pritchard clung to the ropes as she inched her way to the topsail. The noonday tropical sun beat down. Sweat burned her eyes and distracted her. She tried, without success, to wipe her eyes on her shoulder. Hannah's hands burned on the rough lines, as she had learned the ship's ropes were called, and there were blisters forming on her palms. She bit her lip to keep from crying out as she pulled her body even higher.

She tried to sustain her courage by thinking about how her shipmates made it look so simple. They scampered quickly to the top of the mast. But she had not realized how a brisk wind made the lines twist and sway. Every time she placed her bare foot where the line should be, she discovered that the wind had moved it. Her foot found no place to step. Plus the lines were slippery from the ocean spray, something she had not expected.

She tested the next step with her bare foot. Far below on the deck the men called encouragement. "You can do it, Jack." That was her friend Daniel. "Good lad." This was from John Meyer, another of Hannah's fellow sailors.

Out of the corner of her eye, Hannah saw Mr. Hailey, the second mate, come out of the captain's cabin to watch. His shoulder wound, inflicted by a British sailor during the capture of the ship, was bleeding again. Mr. Hailey was acting captain on the *Majestic*. Part of the crew of the *Sea Hawk*, including Hannah, were sailing the captured *Majestic* back to the *Sea Hawk*'s home port of Portsmouth. The *Sea Hawk* had already captured a British merchant ship loaded with goods to be sold, with the proceeds to be divided among the crew. Mr. Gaines, the first mate, had sailed that ship back several weeks before.

Looking out across the waves, Hannah could see the *Sea Hawk*—smaller, but more beautiful than the *Majestic*—sailing beside them. Mr. Hailey gave commands to bring them close enough for Dobbs, who served as the doctor, to come on board the *Majestic* and rebandage his wound.

Without thinking, Hannah looked down, trying to see Daniel, the only one besides Dobbs who knew that she was a girl. Her vision blurred and she hugged the lines as a wave of nausea passed through her.

"Don't look down," Daniel shouted.

His warning came too late. Hannah's feet slid off the wet ropes, and for one terrifying minute she grimly gripped the ropes while her body swung free. Her hands rubbed painfully raw as she hung high above the deck.

"Stay calm," Daniel called softly.

The weight of her body pulled at her shoulders and she felt her hands slipping, but knowing she was about to die made her angry instead of scared. As a cabin boy, she was not required to climb the ropes. She had only done it because of the crew's teasing. "You'll never be a proper sailor if you can't climb the ropes," they had all said. Even Daniel had encouraged her. Surely, after all she had been through since her adventure began, she was not going to die because of a taunt.

She thought about how Daniel and Ratso, an old sailor she had met aboard the *Sea Hawk*, scurried up the lines. If they could do it, so could she. Determined now, she twisted her body, swinging against the ropes until at last she was able to get a foothold. With one shuddering sigh of relief, she climbed up the last few feet. Holding on tightly, she reached out and pulled the knot, allowing the topsail to unfurl.

"Very good lad," Meyer shouted. "You're a sailor now for true."

Flushed with pride, she climbed down—not as quickly as Daniel and Ratso, but with a respectable sure-footedness.

Daniel grinned at her as she leaped down to the wooden deck. "Perhaps Mr. Hailey will let you take over my job."

Hannah glanced up at the main mast, towering above her. A fall from that height would have killed her, or at least left her terribly injured. "Then you would have to cook," she answered lightly, hoping he did not notice her shaking knees. As always, she was careful to keep her voice low and boyish, so that no one else would know she was a girl. "I think no one would be happy then."

Mr. Hailey leaned against the railing around the quarterdeck. His face was pale and pinched with pain. Even now, Hannah shuddered when she remembered how she had swung her cutlass, cutting off the British officer's hand. But not before he had inflicted a deep cut on Mr. Hailey's shoulder.

"Perhaps you should rest, Sir," Hannah said. "I could bring you some tea."

"Even tea can't disguise the terrible water," Mr. Hailey said. "That English captain was a poor sort to let his men visit the taverns before they had replenished the water supply."

"Good thing for us," Hannah replied. "Or we would not have had the chance to take the ship."

Mr. Hailey smiled thinly. "True enough," he said. "Back to your duties. We will get some fresh water from the *Sea Hawk*, and then you can make me some tea."

"Yes, Sir," Hannah answered briskly. She headed for the hatch leading down to the galley. On the *Sea Hawk*, she had been a cabin boy, helping Dobbs, who was the cook in addition to being the doctor. On the *Majestic*, Hannah had been named cook, and a sailor named Jonesy had been assigned to help her between his other duties.

The galley was similar to the one on the *Sea Hawk*, but larger. The oven was made of brick and several buckets of sand were nearby in case of fire. Hannah had left large hunks of pork to soak out some of their salt. Hannah's nose twitched in distaste as she inspected it. The water in the wooden barrels was slimy and smelled bad. In addition, there were no fresh greens or fruit, so there was little to break the monotony of dried peas or beans and salt pork.

Hearing a soft thump, Hannah realized they had reached the *Sea Hawk*. Jonesy grinned at her. He was almost toothless and the ones remaining were nearly black.

Hannah wondered how he managed to choke down the hardtack, even after soaking them in tea. Hannah knew he often snuck an extra cup of grog to numb the pain of his rotten teeth. He was a good worker, though. He had been a cabin boy when he was younger, so he knew his way around the galley.

"Let's go up and make sure we get at least one barrel of water," Hannah said. "We could give the salt pork one more soaking."

The *Sea Hawk* was dwarfed by the much larger *Majestic*, but she was swift and trim. Hannah could see the animal pens tucked into one corner of the main deck. In addition to helping Dobbs, Hannah's duties on the *Sea Hawk* had included caring for the animals. Captain Nelson kept some goats for milk and chickens for eggs and an occasional Sunday dinner treat.

"Well, Jack," Dobbs called as he climbed on board. "How do you like being cook?"

Hannah was so glad to see her friend she had to resist the urge to run and give him a hug. Dobbs had the leathery skin common of men who had spent their life at sea. He looked stern, but he was kind, and his speech was that of an educated man. Dobbs had guessed that Hannah was a girl but he had kept her secret.

Dobbs inspected Mr. Hailey's wound and looked at several other minor wounds from the brief fight when they had taken the *Majestic*. "I'll need your help, Jack," he said quietly. "That wound needs to be stitched."

Following Dobbs's instructions, Hannah fetched a bowl of fresh water and tore the linen sheet from the

English captain's bed into strips. She helped Mr. Hailey remove his shirt, wincing when she saw the wound. The sword had struck Mr. Hailey between his neck and shoulder. If Hannah had not swung her cutlass, deflecting the blow, Mr. Hailey no doubt would have lost his head.

Out of his box of supplies, Dobbs drew a bottle of rum. Hannah supposed he would give it to Mr. Hailey to drink, but instead he poured a good splash of it over the wound. Mr. Hailey roared with pain, but Dobbs held him down until he had calmed. Then he allowed the second mate to take a few swigs from the bottle.

"Do you know how to sew?" Dobbs asked.

"Y-yes," Hannah admitted. "But not on a person."

Dobbs chuckled. "Nothing to it. Pretend Mr. Hailey here is a quilt."

Hannah started to protest but Dobbs gave her a stern look. "I am strong. I can hold him still," he said. Hannah sighed and picked up the needle. It was already threaded with heavy black thread.

"Tie each stitch off," advised Dobbs. "And make them deep enough to hold."

Taking a deep breath, Hannah plunged the needle into one side of Mr. Hailey's wound. Mr. Hailey yelped and flinched, but Dobbs held him tightly.

Hannah did not like to see anyone in pain. "I'm sorry, Mr. Hailey," she said, forgetting to lower her voice.

Mr. Hailey, fortunately, was too concerned with his own troubles to notice, although Dobbs gave her a warning look. Hannah bent to her work, pulling the wound together with a neat row of twenty stitches. Mr. Dobbs bound it up with the cloth strips. "Fine job, Jack," he said. "With a little luck Mr. Hailey will soon be as good as new."

Leaving Mr. Hailey to rest, Hannah helped Dobbs tend to several other wounds. When they were finished, Hannah leaned against the rail in relief. "The sight of blood makes my legs feel weak," she admitted.

"Fine privateer you are," Dobbs teased.

"I wish I could go back on the *Sea Hawk*," she said.

"That makes two of us," Daniel said, walking up behind them.

Dobbs shaded his eyes from the sun with his hand. "There is an island less than a day's sail from here," he said. "Captain Nelson is going to have the *Majestic* anchor at an island before we head north. According to the charts, it is uninhabited and there is fresh water. The men might not be as happy having Jonesy for a cook, but I'll see what I can do about getting you back on board. Shouldn't be too hard. The animals miss you."

chapter two

Back Home on the *Sea Hawk*

After a short sail the next morning, both ships anchored at a small bay. It was still early in the day but it was already sweltering. A breeze bent the tropical trees, promising rain later but offering little relief from the heat. It was a beautiful island with thick jungle growth almost to the water's edge. Brightly colored fish darted about in a turquoise ocean.

Almost as soon as they dropped anchor, Dobbs made good on his promise and sent a small boat with two men to replace Hannah and Daniel. Mr. Hailey stayed in his cabin. Daniel whispered that he had seen him earlier and he had appeared drunk. "It is a good thing the men know what to do without him," Daniel said. He frowned. "I know Mr. Hailey is wounded, but he should at least show himself. I am glad to be back on the *Sea Hawk*."

Hannah looked out at the small boats going back and forth to the island bringing water, fresh greens, and turtles. Jonesy promised to make the men a good dinner, putting them in a happier mood. “Captain Nelson is a harsh master at times, but perhaps that is necessary to keep a ship running smoothly,” she said.

With only a few pulls on the oars as they headed for the *Sea Hawk*, Hannah was drenched in sweat. The heat seemed to suck the air out of her chest, like she was trying to breathe underwater. Reaching over the side, she splashed water on them both. The water dried quickly, but did give them a moment of relief. They used the winch to bring the boat to the forecastle deck, and tied it securely. Dobbs was not on board to greet them when they arrived. Although the *Sea Hawk* had stocked up at an earlier island, he had gone ashore to fetch more greens and fruit.

“Welcome back aboard,” Captain Nelson called out from the quarterdeck. “Mr. Dobbs tells me he cannot carry on without you, Jack.”

“Thank you for allowing me to return as well, Sir,” Daniel said.

“You can thank Dobbs for your return also.” Captain Nelson’s mouth twitched with a smile. “He said the men will mutiny if they don’t see a championship checkers game soon. It seems there have been a lot of wagers on the outcome.”

"I hope they have wagered on me," Daniel answered with a grin.

"What say you to that, Jack?" asked Captain Nelson.

"It is fine with me if the men have no better use for their money than to throw it away," said Hannah.

Captain Nelson laughed. "Daniel, help Jack clean up the livestock. We are running so shorthanded there will not be much time for games. Perhaps on Sunday. I would like to watch this game myself."

As soon as Hannah was settled in her tiny cabin next to the galley, she went to inspect the animals. The goats greeted her, nudging and nibbling at her clothes through their cages. Her favorite, a goat she had named Mrs. Tibbs, bleated a soft greeting.

"They are glad to see you, boy," said Ratso, clapping her roughly on the back. Ratso had been sailing aboard the *Sea Hawk*. "They have been neglected these last few days."

Hannah set to work cleaning the cages and milking the goats. Daniel helped scour the deck and sprinkle grain for the chickens. Now that they were alone, there was an awkward silence between them. "I'm not sure how to act around you," Daniel admitted, after they had worked a while. Hannah looked up from her scrubbing. "Before you knew I was a girl we were friends. Can't we still be friends?"

Daniel shrugged. "I never had a girl for a friend," he said.

"Well, then forget I am a girl. Just think of me as Jack," Hannah said.

Daniel nodded. "It seems strange, but I will try." He grinned. "So Jack, are you still going to leave the ship when we reach Portsmouth?" Just then Ratso came into view as he worked on a sail.

Hannah rocked back on her heels and wiped the sweat off her brow with her sleeve while she thought of her answer. Making sure to keep her voice low because of Ratso, she said, "When my parents and brother were killed by a British raiding party, I could not think of anything but revenge. Being a privateer seemed like the only way I could do that. I've learned to love the sea, and I'm grateful that I got to see so many beautiful places." She looked out at the pristine island, then picked up her brush and went back to scrubbing. "I do miss the feel of solid land under my feet, but I almost forgot the real reason we are here. I think we are a part of something really important. I don't need revenge anymore, but I do need to see the British driven away and America a country where people are free to rule themselves. So I guess I'm staying with the ship until the war is over." Hannah looked up and blushed when she saw several sailors listening.

"That was a fine speech," said Mr. Carhart, the new first mate. He was tall and thin and he had a habit of twirling the end of his very bushy mustache when he was speaking. He had the air of a gentleman, but when the *Majestic* had been close to the *Sea Hawk*, Hannah had seen him climbing the lines and calmly manning the wheel in a storm. The men respected him and Hannah thought he might be a very good first mate.

"Back to work, men," Mr. Carhart said now. "We've got a ship to sail and, as Jack says, a war to win."

The wind was growing stronger and the *Sea Hawk* rocked in the waves. Captain Nelson paced the deck looking out at the small boats making their way back to the *Majestic* and *Sea Hawk*.

Ratso was sitting by the hatch, smoking a long-stemmed pipe and mending a sail. "There's a hard storm that comes up in this part of the world," he said. "Sometimes it comes on land but mostly it's at sea. They call it a hurricane. Men say the winds go in a circle and at the center of the storm it is perfectly calm. I think Captain Nelson will try to outrun it when all the men return."

Hannah cast a worried look at the sky. She had been through a bad northern storm, and the thought of another filled her with dread. She looked at the island and saw with relief that Dobbs and the men with him were already on their way back to the ship.

She could see the men on shore scrambling to load barrels of fresh water and sacks of fruit on to the small boats from the *Majestic*. Most of the men were seasoned sailors and recognized the danger.

Captain Nelson was already giving orders to sail the minute that Dobbs and his men reached the *Sea Hawk*. Hannah ran to help bring on the fresh supplies. Daniel was already at the winch, helping to raise the heavy anchor. There was urgency in the sailors' movements but they did their jobs with quiet efficiency. As the sails caught the wind Hannah looked back at the *Majestic*. It had not yet pulled up its anchor. Several boats had not yet made it back. The wind was quite brisk now. White foam capped the waves. The sky was still a clear blue, although Hannah could see a roll of dark clouds on the horizon.

Hannah and Dobbs dragged several heavy bags down the hatch to the galley. "Do you think the storm will hit us?" Hannah asked.

"Captain will try to stay ahead of it," Dobbs shrugged. "Won't help to fret about it."

George, the ship's orange cat, wound himself around Hannah's legs and she stooped to pet him. "Did you miss me?" Hannah said as she stroked him.

"He's been meowing since you left," Dobbs chuckled. "Probably hasn't caught a single rat, he was so upset."

A cauldron of salted beef and pease already bubbled on the stove. Dobbs pointed to a large bag. "That is full of greens. Mix some up for the crew." Hannah sorted through the greens, cutting them into bite-sized pieces. She tossed in several handfuls of berries that Dobbs had found on the island and cut small wedges of cheese. Over the top, she drizzled oil and vinegar. Dobbs gave an approving glance.

"I learned to make greens this way when I worked at the Inn," Hannah told him.

"The men will think they have died and gone to heaven. I'm making some flummery for dessert."

On the lid of the cauldron, he set a smaller pan to cook flour, oatmeal, suet, and raisins. He stirred in a few precious spices for flavor. The ship rocked gently while they worked, and Hannah could feel that it was moving swiftly, blown by the storm.

Two sailors from the first watch came to the galley and Dobbs dished up portions into smaller buckets. Hannah set out a tray for the captain. When she stepped out of the hatch, she could see the ominous gray cloud boiling in the sky behind them. Above the ship the sky was still blue.

She found Captain Nelson sitting at his desk, studying charts with a worried frown. He looked up and smiled. "Good to have you back, lad."

"Thank you, Sir," Hannah answered. "I am glad to be back. The English ship is magnificent, but the *Sea Hawk* is like home."

Captain Nelson sipped at his tea as she set out his meal. "I know that you wanted revenge for what the British and Tories did to your family," he said. "I am told that you conducted yourself quite admirably. Did that satisfy your need for revenge?"

Hannah paused, still holding the wooden tray. "It did not bring back my parents," she answered slowly. "I do feel proud to help win our freedom from the British."

"Well said, Jack." Captain Nelson nodded. "We have done well. If we can get past this storm and back to port, we will have helped our country and made ourselves rich." He glanced out his windows frowning. "Mr. Hailey has too much space between us," he muttered, more to himself than her. "We will lose each other in the dark." He waved his arm, dismissing Hannah. "Tie down the animals well, Jack. It could be a rough night."

Hannah hastened to do as Captain Nelson ordered, making sure the cages were tightly secured in their spot on the deck, and then covering them with canvas. Captain Nelson paced the quarterdeck, stopping occasionally to scan the horizon with a small telescope, which he called "a glass." Ratso and Daniel were working up in the sails as the captain shouted orders to them, trying to keep the ship ahead of the storm.

"What took you so long?" Dobbs growled when she returned to the galley.

Hannah explained about the animals. "I think the wind is blowing the ship off course," she said as she started scrubbing pots. "Captain Nelson is worried that the *Majestic* is too far away."

Dobbs shook his head. "Hailey's a fool. Moreover, the men don't respect him. We'll be lucky if he makes it back to port."

They worked together, putting the galley in order for the next meal. Dobbs insisted that the galley be cleaned each day. The wind was growing stronger and the ship rose and fell with the rolling waves.

"We'll have to let the fire go out," Dobbs said. "The wind is getting too rough. We'll just have biscuits and cheese tonight."

Hannah nodded. She had not been seasick since her first week at sea, but the constant rolling of the ship was beginning to make her stomach churn.

"Go fetch more wood for the stove," Dobbs said. "We might as well use this time to stock up."

Hannah sighed. Getting wood from the dark smelly hold was her least favorite thing to do. It took her four trips to fill the box to Dobbs's satisfaction.

When she was finished, Dobbs said, "Go up and get some air." He looked at her pale face. "You don't look so good."

Hannah climbed up to the main deck. Although the ship was still pitching wildly, the fresh air soon revived her. Daniel and Ratso were nowhere in sight. They had been replaced on the sails by two other sailors.

Captain Nelson insisted that anyone on deck had to be working, except for Sunday afternoons. Hannah looked around for a chore to keep herself busy. She was pleased when she spied Daniel and Ratso sitting in a sheltered corner between the securely fastened boats, braiding rope. Daniel looked up and grinned. "I was telling Ratso how we are going to be partners and have a farm someday."

"How do you know you would like that, Daniel?" Hannah asked seriously. "It's a lot of work. And it can be lonely."

"I lived in the city," Daniel said, with a melancholy look on his face. "People threw their garbage and dumped their chamber pots in the streets. My father worked twelve hours a day, and could just barely feed his family. Every few months sickness would sweep through the street, killing many. My mother and father died in a smallpox epidemic. At least on a farm the air would be clean. I'm not afraid of work. And I wouldn't mind being lonely. Not if I was working on my own land."

"I've been at sea almost my whole life," Ratso said thoughtfully. "Maybe I should buy me a bit of land too. Might be I could find me a widow woman who would like to marry a handsome fellow like myself." A few drops of rain began to fall, and the sailors hurried their work.

Hannah and Daniel exchanged a look. They were both fond of the old sailor.

"You could come with us," Daniel said.

For a brief second Ratso's face lit up with a smile. Then he laughed. "You two young fellows wouldn't want an old salt like me."

Before anyone else could speak, the few drops of rain turned into a curtain of water, drenching them. The wind blew the rain so hard that it stung their skin, but even that did not break the suffocating heat.

They quickly coiled the new rope and dashed to fasten down all the hatches.

"You two man the bilge pumps," Mr. Carhart shouted over the noise of the rain, gesturing at Hannah and Daniel.

They pumped for the next hour, trying to stay ahead of the water that the ship was taking in. Slimy, putrid water splashed up and over their bare feet before it drained over the side. There were rotted bodies of dead rats and some things Hannah could not even identify. "I've never smelled anything so bad," she gasped, trying to keep from gagging.

Daniel paused pumping long enough to grin at her misery. "If you were in the crew's quarters you would smell this every day," he teased.

"More pumping, less talking!" Mr. Carhart yelled.

Hannah bent to her work. Her hands were soon blistered and bleeding and the muscles in her shoulders ached. At last, when she thought she could bear no more, two other sailors relieved her and Daniel. "I'm going to sleep while I have the chance," Daniel said as he headed for his hammock. Hannah hurried to the galley, wincing when she tried to move her hands.

"Let me see," Dobbs said, noticing her pained expression. He inspected her hands without further comment. Then he ordered her to sit. He fetched salve from the medicine chest, and rubbed some on her hands.

"Better get some sleep," he said.

Hannah could not imagine sleeping with the ship pitching wildly, but by the time she had toweled herself dry and changed clothes, she was yawning. The salve had soothed her hands. She flipped up in her hammock and wrapped herself in her blanket. George the cat hopped up and settled beside her, ready for a good petting. She had only given him a couple of strokes when her eyes closed and she was asleep.

chapter three

At the Edge of the Hurricane

The sailors all had tales to tell of hurricanes—ships capsized with all hands lost, ships blown clear up onto land. Under Captain Nelson's expert command, however, the *Sea Hawk* managed to stay just ahead of the storm. The crew did not escape the torrential rains, which continued for the next three days. Between the rains, the heat was relentless and exhausting. Belowdecks it was even worse, making it difficult to breathe and impossible to sleep. Hannah almost wished they had been caught in the hurricane. At least that way the storm might have been over quickly. As it was, everyone was wet and gloomy, and tempers, from the heat and lack of sleep, were short. Several fights broke out, but the sailors had escaped punishment because neither Mr. Carhart nor Captain Nelson had witnessed them. Hannah wondered if they had simply chosen not to see, since Captain Nelson missed very little that happened on his ship.

Hannah's clothes were constantly wet and it did no good to change to her other outfit because even belowdecks it was too damp for them to dry. The crew's quarters reeked with the odor of soaked wood, clothes, and slimy bilge water. The rain was so heavy that the pumps had to be manned almost around the clock. Hannah had taken several more turns at the pumps in between her regular chores.

All this time they did not see another ship, although someone was aloft constantly peering through the glass, hoping for a glimpse of the *Majestic*. After the third day, the rain ceased, but the sky remained overcast. There was a good wind, however, so although the lower decks remained damp and miserable, the boards on all of the decks began to dry. They had been swollen with water, but as they dried they shrank and warped, opening gaps between them. Hannah helped Mr. Bowden, the ship's carpenter, repair the boards with tar. If the gaps were large they pressed rope or wadding inside the gaps before adding the tar.

The ship was so shorthanded that everyone had to do extra duty. But everyone's spirits improved with the better weather and the thought of the treasure they would share at the end of the voyage. Men who had been at each other's throats only a day before now joked as they worked and discussed plans for their newfound wealth.

One evening, just before dusk, Hannah was hurrying from the galley with dinner for Captain Nelson and Mr. Carhart when she heard a boom that sounded like cannon fire. She paused, listening. Hearing no other sound, she told herself it was only the thunder of a distant storm.

Captain Nelson came out of his cabin and called to Ratso, who was on watch, "Do you see anything?"

Ratso twisted in the ropes to scan in every direction. "No, Sir, perhaps it was only thunder," he shouted.

"Perhaps," answered the captain, looking truly unconvinced.

After a minute of listening, the captain went back into his cabin. He looked at his charts with a frown while Hannah laid out his supper. Even the roast chicken did not seem to cheer him up. Mr. Carhart, though, dug into his meal with gusto.

"I saw a seagull this afternoon," Hannah ventured. "Are we close to land?"

Captain Nelson pointed on the charts to a long narrow island along the coast. "The storm has blown us closer to land than I would like," he said. "This is a barrier island, nearly a hundred miles long. It runs along the coast of the Carolinas. We will be passing it soon. No doubt that is where your gull came from. There are British in these waters. I didn't think we would be challenged sailing with the *Majestic*, but we seem to have lost her."

"There are lots of coves and places to hide, if we are chased," Mr. Carhart offered.

Captain Nelson nodded. "These waters can be treacherous though. Ships have run aground and sunk."

Later, Hannah repeated the conversation to Dobbs. "Captain Nelson is a good captain," Dobbs said. "That's more than can be said about Mr. Hailey."

Later that evening Mr. Carhart called for all hands on deck. As soon as they were assembled, Captain Nelson addressed them. "We have been blown off course by the hurricane," he admitted. "I believe we're close to the Carolina shore. The British are active in these waters, but perhaps we can sneak by them. We are going to run up an English flag and pretend to be an English merchant ship. If we can make it back, we will all be rich men."

Captain Nelson paced the quarterdeck, as though collecting his thoughts while the men waited. "The *Sea Hawk* is a good ship. If we are attacked, we may be able to outrun them. We only have enough sailors to man five guns, but we have plenty of powder," he said. "I do not fancy rotting on some British prison ship, but I will leave the decision to you. If it comes to it, shall we fight or surrender?"

"Fight!" the men roared. Hannah cheered with them, trying to ignore the icy clutch of fear in her stomach.

Captain Nelson nodded. "This is the finest crew I have had the privilege to lead. Now, I want all guns ready and loaded, with two extra cartridges of powder by each one. Gun captains, practice with your crews. Jack and Daniel, you will be the powder runners. Mr. Carhart will show you what to do."

Suddenly everyone had a task to perform. Mr. Carhart led Hannah and Daniel to the magazine deep in the hold. There a sailor passed premeasured felt bags of powder through a wet curtain. Mr. Carhart showed them how to enclose the bags in a leather carrying case. "Make sure your case is fastened securely," he warned. "One spark could blow you to smithereens."

Cold fear clutched at Hannah, making her legs feel weak. But she tried to put the danger out of her mind as she raced beside Daniel up the stairs, holding the powder case. She delivered the powder to her assigned three-man gun crew, and then sprinted back down for more. "Faster, faster," Mr. Carhart screamed. "In a real battle each gun will need a bag every three minutes."

"Are you scared, lad?" Ratso asked, when they were finally allowed to rest.

"A little," Hannah admitted.

"Good," the old man said grimly. "That will keep you careful. I saw a powder monkey get blown up once. Wasn't enough left to bury."

Daniel looked a little pale. "Do you really think we will have to fight?"

Ratso shrugged but, before he could reply, Mr. Carhart approached them. "Get some sleep, men," he said.

Hannah was only too happy to comply. They headed for the hatches—Ratso and Daniel to the crew quarters—and Hannah to her tiny room next to the galley. Every muscle in her body screamed in protest from the trips up and down to the powder magazine. She groaned as she rolled into her hammock to rest. In spite of her aches, she felt hopeful as she closed her eyes. The practice had gone smoothly and Captain Nelson was a good captain. He would get them safely back to port.

Hannah slept fitfully, unable to get comfortable because of her sore muscles. At sunrise, even before she opened her eyes, Hannah sensed something had changed. Her feet were already on the floor before she realized that it was the silence that had awakened her. No, she told herself. Not total silence. She could still hear the creaking of the masts, the flap of sails, and the thumps of men's feet on the deck above her. But the sound was muffled like snowy winter mornings on the farm. She opened her door and peeked out into the galley.

Dobbs was already up, setting a tray for the captain. "Ah. Awake are you? Captain Nelson just sent for some tea. He's been up all night."

Hannah listened again to the strange silence. "Has something happened?"

"Storm has blown us close to the coast and the fog is so thick you can't see your hand held up in front of you." Dobbs cut several wedges of cheese and put them on a tray with some of the fruit he had found on the island. "Go on. Take it to him. Mind your step."

Clutching the tray, Hannah pushed open the hatch. Tendrils of fog swirled down the hatchway stairs. Another step up the hatch and she was completely enveloped in a thick, white fog.

Hannah stood for a minute to get her bearings. A faint glow came from the wheel, where Captain Nelson was giving orders to a sailor. Another sailor stood at the end of the deck, dropping a long, weighted rope over the side and calling out the readings.

The sea was calmer and Hannah thought they might have outrun the storm. However, she knew from the tense sound of the captain's voice that they were still in grave danger.

Using the faint lantern glow as a beacon and balancing the tray, Hannah felt her way across the deck. The fog swirled around her feet, making it impossible to see where she walked. She reached the steps to the quarterdeck, breathing a sigh of relief that she had not stumbled and dropped the tray. She set it down and poured a cup of tea from the pot. The captain took it absently and sipped, still concentrating on the man at the wheel.

The sun was coming up. Hannah could see the red glow on the horizon. A sudden breeze blew, chilling her. At the same instant, she heard Daniel's shout from the main mast. "Ship ahoy, Captain!"

"Can you see who it is?" Captain Nelson called back.

Daniel didn't answer for a minute, and then as another breeze blew he called down, "It's a frigate. I can't tell if it is the *Majestic*, but it looks like it."

"Keep watch," Captain Nelson said. "Let me know when you can see her name." Holding his mug of tea, he anxiously paced the quarterdeck.

Hannah tended to the animals, all the while watching Daniel as he tried to catch a better look at the ship through the thick fog. The rising sun cast a soft red glow, but it would be several hours before it was warm enough to burn off the fog. She lingered at the animal cages, hoping to hear Daniel call out the good news that the ship was indeed the *Majestic*.

"Can you see the name?" Captain Nelson called several times.

"It is the *Majestic*," Daniel called finally.

"Well thanks be for that," Captain Nelson said, looking relieved. Several sailors on deck gave a cheer.

Hannah hurried down to the galley and relayed the news to Dobbs.

He looked pleased. "That should make the rest of the voyage easy. The English Navy will think we are being escorted, and the merchants will stay away from the *Majestic*."

"Why would they stay away?" Hannah asked.

"The English Navy can board any merchant ship and take men to be part of their crew. The merchant captain can't stop them because it's their law. The men are practically prisoners. They are not allowed out when the ship is at port, and if they try to escape they can be shot."

"That's not fair!" Hannah said.

Dobbs shrugged. "The English Navy ships have huge crews. I guess that's the only way they can get enough men. Life aboard one of them is harsh. Men are flogged or even hanged for the slightest infraction."

"I'm glad I am on the *Sea Hawk*," Hannah said.

"She's a good ship," Dobbs agreed. "Now let's get the men fed before they mutiny."

chapter four

Battle

Shortly before sunset, Hannah finally had a chance to go back up on deck. She headed for one of the two ship bathrooms, called heads, grateful as always that the *Sea Hawk* had them enclosed, instead of out in the open like most ships. The *Majestic*'s heads were exposed. Hannah had been forced to relieve herself only at night, or in a bucket she hid in the hold.

Now that the fog was gone she could see the faint outline of land on the horizon. A steady westerly wind was still pushing them in that direction.

The jubilation that she had observed only a few hours ago seemed to have disappeared and she looked around for the reason. Two large frigates bearing the English flag were heading straight for them at full sail.

The *Majestic* was much closer now, but Captain

Nelson appeared grim as he paced the deck. Holding the speaking horn, he called, "Mr. Hailey. Can you hear me?"

There was no answer. A minute later he called again, "Ahoy, the *Majestic*."

After a tense interval Mr. Hailey appeared on the *Majestic*'s quarterdeck. "I can hear you," he shouted into his own speaking horn. His words were slurred, and Hannah wondered if he was drunk.

Captain Nelson hesitated, perhaps coming to the same conclusion. "Do you understand what you are to say? The *Sea Hawk* is headed with supplies to the garrisons in New York and the *Majestic* is escorting her."

"What if they don't believe me?" Mr. Hailey's voice had a whiny edge.

"Make them believe you," Captain Nelson roared. "Tell them you are on a special mission for General Howe."

"I'll try," Mr. Hailey called back.

"Have some of your men put on the British uniforms. Get your gun crews ready in case there is trouble. This should have been done already," Captain Nelson bellowed, eyeing the rapidly approaching English ships. "I expect you to do your duty."

"Yes, Sir," Mr. Hailey said.

Hannah could not believe what was happening. She saw her fear mirrored in the other sailors' eyes.

"The first ship is hailing the *Majestic*," the sailor on the mast shouted. The entire crew of the *Sea Hawk* held their breath. The ships were too far away to hear the conversation. The second ship continued toward the *Sea Hawk*. Turning away from the *Majestic*, Captain Nelson and Mr. Carhart started shouting orders. The second enemy ship was turning so that in a few minutes she would cross the *Sea Hawk*'s stern.

Suddenly, from the *Majestic* came a terrifying boom. Hannah could see one of the masts on the English ship crack and fall.

"That fool Hailey has thrown us into battle," Captain Nelson cursed and started shouting orders to keep the English ship from crossing the stern. Hannah understood that if the ship fired on them from that position the cannon could destroy the whole length of the hull.

Suddenly Ratso was beside her. "Courage, lad," he whispered.

"Can't we try to outrun their ship?" Hannah asked frantically.

Ratso shook his head. "They've got us trapped against the land. Any closer and we could run aground." He looked at the red sun low in the horizon. "Maybe we can escape in the dark, if we can hold them off that long."

"To your guns," shouted Mr. Carhart.

Hannah stood frozen in terror as the gun crews raced to their positions. Mr. Carhart gave her a shove. "Powder," he yelled. "Move."

Hannah moved without even thinking. She passed Daniel already heading up with his bag of powder. She raced down and grabbed her own powder sack and stuffed it into the protective case, fastening it with shaking hands.

Just as she started up the steps there was another boom. The *Sea Hawk* shuddered, and Hannah stumbled, nearly losing her footing. She raced up, nearly running into Daniel, who was already on his way down again. "Hurry," he yelled.

"Fire when ready," Mr. Carhart called.

One of the sailors grabbed the powder, and Hannah set off again, just as the *Sea Hawk*'s guns were fired. The tremendous roar of the guns sent a pain through her head that deafened her.

Hannah had just delivered the third powder bag when there was a loud roar. The force of the blast knocked her off her feet. A cannonball had torn through the area between two guns, sending splinters of wood—some as big as a man's hand—flying through the air. A sailor let out a horrible scream and clutched his face. A jagged piece of wood at least two inches wide protruded from his eye socket and blood streamed down from the wound.

Two sailors assisted the wounded man to the hospital area Dobbs had set up at one end of the crew's quarters.

Hannah picked herself up, surprised that she was not wounded. Three men near her were bleeding profusely from splinters embedded in their arms, legs, and chests. Gamely they turned back to their gun, preparing to fire.

Hannah scrambled back down to the magazine, making trip after trip up to the gun deck. On one trip the men, still bleeding, were cheering, and she allowed herself a moment of hope. She caught a glimpse of the *Majestic* through the gaping hole left by the cannonball. It was almost nighttime, but she could see the fire of the ship's blazing guns. Mr. Hailey seemed to be putting up a good fight.

Now that the battle was actually raging, Hannah moved automatically, focused only on the job at hand, forcing fear to the back of her mind. Hannah was so weary she was numb, but she willed herself to keep moving in spite of her exhaustion. Daniel looked equally fatigued, but he managed a smile as they passed. Hannah was vaguely aware of the captain shouting orders, setting the sails to maneuver the ship into a more advantageous position. Mr. Carhart paced the gun deck shouting orders and encouragement, until there was another terrible roar of a cannonball. Suddenly, the top half of the first mate was gone. The bottom part of him stood for a second, spilling blood and intestines before it simply tumbled to the floor.

Hannah retched and staggered to the rail. She felt Daniel's strong hand holding her. "Put it out of your mind," he said quietly. "It was mercifully quick."

Hannah stared at the carnage, trying to contain her horror. For the first time since the fight began, she became aware of the terrible damage to the *Sea Hawk*. The captain's cabin had been hit, and the main mast broken nearly in two. The deck was slippery with blood. Men she had served breakfast to that morning lay dead or dying. The ship was listing badly, and she knew it would soon sink.

"Jack, Daniel," Captain Nelson called, "I have a job for the two of you."

"Should we get more powder?" Daniel wondered.

Captain Nelson ordered two sailors to take over the powder runs. He paused, listening as the two men scrambled down to the magazine. From the British ship came a faint call. "Heave ho, and let us board. Surrender now and you will be treated fairly. You have five minutes to decide."

Ignoring the call, Captain Nelson turned to Daniel and Hannah. "Help me carry the chest in my quarters to the ship's boat." Without waiting to see if they were following, he picked his way through the rubble and tattered sails littering the deck.

They climbed past the animal cages and Hannah let out a small cry. In the chaos she had forgotten to take the animals to safety below deck. The cages were smashed and all the animals were dead save for Mrs. Tibbs, standing by the crushed cages, trembling with fear.

The captain's beautiful cabin was nothing but splinters. Glass from the large windows had shattered across the room, making it treacherous to walk. Seeing the danger for their bare feet, Captain Nelson motioned for them to stop.

Captain Nelson searched in a corner, lifting several pieces of wood, and finally pulling out two pairs of boots.

"They'll be too big for you, but at least you won't cut your feet to shreds."

Gratefully, Hannah and Daniel pulled them on. They helped move rubble, freeing the chest, which was amazingly undamaged. With a protesting howl, George crawled out of the debris, fur standing on end and his eyes wide with fright. Captain Nelson scooped him up, lifted the lid of the chest and deposited him on top of the coins.

"Hurry," the captain said. They lifted the chest and picked their way across the ship to the forecastle deck where the ship's boats were tied. Inside the chest George continued to screech.

One of the boats was damaged, but still looked seaworthy. The others had remained unharmed.

"Lower the boats on the starboard side where the ship will shield you from view," Captain Nelson said, just as

Ratso—a large bandage wrapped around his arm and another on his head—and Dobbs appeared at the hatchway.

"Go with these two. Land is no more than five miles away. Hide the chest. At least the men who survive will have something for this terrible day." From inside his shirt he brought out a ledger and handed it to Dobbs. "Make sure the widows get a share."

The guns on the *Sea Hawk* had fallen silent. Hannah knew there were not enough men left to fire them.

"What about you, Captain?" Dobbs asked gently.

"I'll be on the second boat with the rest of the men. I want you men that I trust to have a head start to hide the treasure."

Dobbs nodded. He put out his hand. "It's been a pleasure to serve with you, Captain Nelson."

Captain Nelson nodded. "You've been a good crew. Now, go! Time is running out."

Daniel was already at the winch, lowering the boat. Dobbs was silent as they worked. His clothes were drenched in the blood of the men who had died that day. In spite of his efforts, their wounds had been too grievous. Hannah had heard their moans and screams as she delivered her powder. Much more fortunate were the ones who had died instantly, like Mr. Carhart.

The captain had disappeared. There was a boom and a cannonball splashed into the water, missing them by only a few feet. “Go,” Dobbs said tersely. Suddenly Hannah dashed back to the petrified Mrs. Tibbs and gathered her up just as another round shattered what remained of the captain’s cabin.

Dobbs cursed. “We are about to die and you’re saving a little goat?”

Choosing that moment to come out of her frightened stupor, Mrs. Tibbs struggled as Hannah climbed down the rope ladder, but Ratso reached up, grabbed the animal, and dumped it into the boat.

Dobbs was still muttering when he got in the boat. “A goat. A goat. Twenty men are dead and he saves a goat.”

“Ahh, leave the lad be,” Ratso soothed. “He couldn’t save the twenty men.”

Dobbs grunted, and picked up the oars. Hannah held Mrs. Tibbs, crooning softly to calm her. Daniel unhooked the boat. “Does anyone know which way to get to land?” he asked.

It was completely dark and a thin fog was already forming over the water. The acrid smell of gunpowder hung in the air, mixing with the fog and burning in Hannah’s nose when she breathed. It was impossible to get their bearings because the fog and smoke hid the stars. The only light came from the cannons as they fired. It was too dark to see the land and Captain Nelson had maneuvered the *Sea Hawk* into a different position during the battle.

A stray cannonball splashed uncomfortably close, sending up a plume of icy water. "Row," Dobbs said urgently. "Let's get away while we still can. We'll worry about direction later."

Daniel picked up the other oars and the little boat moved away from the battle. Hannah held onto the goat, who seemed to finally accept her fate and curled against the chest of Spanish doubloons. Inside the chest, George continued to complain. Hannah lifted the lid a crack. "You are better off in there, George," she said. "At least you're dry." George sniffed at the opening. Being close to Hannah seemed to calm him and he was silent at last. She wedged a doubloon under the lid to provide some air to the chest.

The small boat was no match for the sea. Waves tossed the boat about, drenching the four desperate sailors and filling the bottom of the boat with water. The distance slowly widened between the sailors and the raging battle, but the smell of burning gunpowder still hung over them.

In the dark, Hannah could barely see the hulk that had been the beautiful *Sea Hawk*. She could just make out several figures climbing down the rope ladder to the second boat. Someone—she thought it was Captain Nelson but she couldn't be sure—stood at the rail.

Suddenly there was a rumble like faraway thunder and a burst of flame. In the brief shaft of light Hannah saw the man at the rail blown into the sea.

"He was a fair captain," Ratso said after a minute of stunned silence.

"The ones in the boat might save him," Daniel said. But it was hard for Hannah to believe that could be true.

Dobbs pulled in his oars. "We have to think about saving ourselves. For all we know, we are heading out to the open sea."

"I've been thinking on that," Ratso said. "I was up in the sails most of the day. Last I saw, land was that way," he said pointing to the left. "Of course, I was below for a time getting bandaged up."

Dobbs glanced up at the overcast sky. "It's too cloudy and dark to even find the North Star. I guess that's as good a way as any."

"We'll take turns on the oars," Dobbs continued, just as another wave splashed over them. "Jack, you'd better grab something and bail. The water is getting deep."

Hannah groped around the bottom of the boat, but there was nothing. Then with a bit of inspiration she pulled off one of her oversized boots.

"Good thinking, Jack," Ratso chuckled.

The wind blew cold against Hannah's wet clothes. She looked around as she scooped out the water, one bootful at a time. She could no longer see, or even hear the signs of the battle. There was no sign of land. There was nothing but darkness and the ocean surrounding them.

It was almost morning when Daniel pulled in his oars. Several times during the long night they had changed positions, Hannah rowing and Daniel bailing, but Dobbs had doggedly manned his oars all night. Ratso was too wounded to row, but he took a few turns at bailing until Dobbs made him rest.

"Do you smell that?" Daniel asked.

Dobbs sniffed. "I don't smell anything but seawater."

Hannah breathed in deeply. "I smell it too. Green things. Trees, grass."

Ratso chuckled. "I think you young folks are having farmer delusions."

"I don't smell anything now," Daniel said, breathing in deeply.

Dobbs pulled in his oars and examined his raw hands. "Let's rest a bit. It should be light soon."

They drifted in silence too weary to talk. Dobbs closed his eyes, and his head fell forward as he drifted off to sleep. Hannah's mouth was dry, and she was hungry. Even though she was exhausted, her mind was in too much turmoil to sleep. What if the island had no food or water? Even if they found land, they might not survive. She looked over at Daniel, realizing that she could see him. It was almost daybreak.

Hannah was so tired she laid her head down on the edge

of the boat. “Are we going to make it, do you think?” she murmured to Daniel.

“Yes,” Daniel said fiercely. “We haven’t gone through all this to die drifting about in a little boat.”

Hannah nodded, pretending that she believed him. In her own mind, she was not so sure. Fighting her fear, she closed her eyes and drifted off to a restless sleep. It was a brief rest, however. In just a few short minutes she awoke to find water rising over her feet and legs. The small boat was being pounded with waves, tossing back and forth. She groped for the boot, floating loose in the bottom of the boat to bail away some of the water. As she reached for the boot she bumped into Ratso. The old man groaned. She felt his head under the bandage. The old man was burning with fever.

She saw Daniel looking at her and shook her head. “He’s sick,” she said helplessly. “We need to get him to land and get him dry.”

Dobbs was awake as well. Twisting around he looked in every direction. “Nothing,” he said dully. “We have gone in the wrong direction or got turned about in the night.”

He squinted at the sky. The glow of the sun was obscured by the heavy clouds, but faint streaks of pink trimmed the clouds to one side. “There has got to be land to the west,” he said. “We will just have to keep rowing.”

chapter five

Marooned

The salty seawater burned Hannah's stiff blistered hands. She was hungry, and the rolling motion of the boat was making her sick, but it was the thirst that bothered her the most. Her tongue felt swollen and her lips were parched and cracked. She kept silent about her complaints, knowing her companions were suffering too.

Daniel picked up the other oars without a word. Using the boot, Hannah bailed as fast as she could, but the waves were getting higher, causing more water to splash into the boat. Mrs. Tibbs stood uneasily, balancing against the side of the boat. Her eyes rolled in terror, and now and then she gave a piteous bleat. Inside the chest George meowed and screeched.

"The animals are miserable," Daniel said.

Dobbs grunted. "Don't waste your sympathy on them. You are going to need it for yourself if we don't see land soon. If those waves get any higher they are likely to capsize us."

Save for the grunts of the two men fighting against the turbulent ocean and the cries of the unhappy animals, the little boat was silent. Hannah did her part, dipping bootful after bootful of water, stopping only to check Ratso and to keep the unconscious man from drowning in the bottom of the boat.

Suddenly Daniel broke the rhythm of the rowing. "I saw land!" Daniel's excited cry caused Dobbs to put up his own oars and stare across the white-foamed waves.

Hannah, too, looked in the direction Daniel was pointing. For a long moment there was hopeful silence and then Dobbs picked up his oars again.

"I see nothing," he said flatly.

Daniel picked up his own oars, but he continued to peer into the distance. "There," he said after a few more minutes of rowing.

"I see it!" Hannah exclaimed. Far off was the unmistakable rise of a sand dune and a few scrubby trees.

"I told you land was that way," Ratso exclaimed gleefully.

"You're awake!" Hannah smiled at the old sailor.

"It takes more than a few cannonballs to keep this old salt down." He struggled to sit up, wincing with pain.

"Rest, old man," Dobbs said as Ratso reached for the other boot. "We'll be on land soon."

As they got closer to the island, Dobbs said glumly, "Looks to me like we got turned around during the night. We have been rowing parallel to the island for no telling how long."

The island stretched in front of them as far as the eye could see in either direction. "At least we didn't head out to the open sea," Hannah said.

"You had better hold on to your little friend there," Dobbs said, pointing to Mrs. Tibbs. The little animal scrambled about as though she sensed how near she was to land and would swim the rest of the way.

"Poor thing, she's probably starving," Hannah said.

"The goat will probably have better luck than anyone finding food," Dobbs said.

From inside the chest George began to meow. "George too," Dobbs said. "If any ships have landed here, there will be rats."

The wind picked up as a sudden squall sent rain stinging against their skin. The wind and waves threatened to dash them onto a rocky shore. The little boat was carried high on the crest of a wave, miraculously not capsizing. Dobbs and Daniel tried to guide the boat, but the waves picked them up over and over again, each time bringing them closer to the rocks. Holding on to Mrs. Tibbs and

Ratso, Hannah crouched helplessly in the bottom of the small boat.

There was a sickening crunch as the bottom of the boat was scraped along some rocks. Water poured into the gash at an alarming rate, but a last huge wave lifted the boat and deposited it at the edge of a small sandy beach. Hannah jumped out with Dobbs and Daniel. Together they managed to pull the boat out of the water. It was still raining, but Hannah was so grateful to be on solid ground that she almost cheered.

Mrs. Tibbs hopped nimbly out of the boat and shook herself as though she too could not believe the joy of land. She scrambled across the sandy beach to a copse of trees. Pulling off a mouthful of leaves, she chewed, oblivious of the rain.

Hannah opened the chest and freed George. With a plaintive howl, George ran to the trees and disappeared.

"Let's get that chest safe before we do anything else," Dobbs said. He walked over to the brush where Mrs. Tibbs, calm after her ordeal, was busily stripping a small shrub of leaves.

"Here looks as good as any place," Dobbs said.

"How would anyone find it again?" Daniel asked, looking both ways on the sandy beach. Small stands of scrubby brush dotted the landscape of shifting dunes, with nothing to distinguish them.

"I've got an idea about that," Ratso said, taking out a knife from a scabbard fastened around his waist. "Bring me two boards, as flat as you can find," he said to Hannah.

She was curious about what the old man had in mind, but she quickly moved to do as he asked. She walked up and down the beach looking at driftwood tossed up by the storm. The rain had stopped almost as quickly as it had started, and the wind was blowing away the last of the storm. Streaks of sunlight shot like arrows through the clouds. She finally found two ship's boards, sanded smooth by the sea and white from the sun, and carried them back to Ratso.

Daniel and Dobbs had dragged the chest inland, near a small growth of brush and sea grass. They were scraping out a hole with two crooked pieces of driftwood and their bare hands. Hannah searched about until she found another piece of driftwood, strong enough to use as a digging tool, and set about helping.

It took several hours to dig a hole big enough to fit the chest inside. Before they covered it, Dobbs reached inside the chest and carefully withdrew eight of the coins and set them aside. "No telling what might happen to us," he said. "We'll each take two coins. Hide them in your clothing."

Hannah folded hers carefully into the sash she wore around her waist, and Daniel did the same. Dobbs tucked his in a small pouch he wore around his neck, under his shirt. Setting Ratso's share aside, they bent to the work of covering the chest.

"Wait," Dobbs suddenly yelled. Reaching inside his shirt, he removed the ledger Captain Nelson had given him and put it in the chest.

When the chest was almost covered, Dobbs broke off several branches and handed them to Hannah and Daniel. "The wind will soon cover our tracks, but smooth them out just in case."

Looking back to the beach, Hannah could see the unmistakable signs of a heavy object dragged into the brush. She and Daniel whisked the sand, working their way back to Ratso, who still sat on the beach near where they had landed.

Grinning broadly, Ratso held up two boards in the shape of a cross. Carved into one of the two boards were the words, "Here lies John Brown. Died of the smallpox."

Hannah clapped her hands in delight. "That is so clever," she said. "Not even a grave robber would dig up someone with smallpox. And we will have a marker when we come back."

Hannah could scarcely hide her alarm when Ratso unwound the bandage from his head revealing a red and swollen wound. Oblivious to her shock, he tore off a bloody strip, and smiling, handed it to her. "They will need something to bind the boards." Nodding wordlessly, she and Daniel took the boards and cloth back to Dobbs.

By the time she got back, Dobbs was patting the ground where they had buried the chest. Dobbs smiled when he saw Ratso's grave marker. "That should keep people away. I just hope we can find it again."

Hannah looked around trying to memorize the few landmarks. A few old Oak trees, bent and stunted from the wind, were nearby, but she suspected there were places like this all over the island. Unlike the tropical islands they had visited, this island seemed to be mostly sand and wind.

"We need water," Hannah said, licking her parched lips. They tasted of salt.

"And food," Daniel said. "I am starving."

Dobbs looked down on the beach where Ratso still sat at the edge of the water. "There are long stretches of deserted land, but the charts showed a few small villages on the island," Dobbs said. "I don't know where we are, although if we head north we are bound to find something. Trouble is, I don't think Ratso can make it."

Daniel looked at the sky and frowned. "I am not sure I can make it very far without resting. Why don't we make camp? We can tip the boat on its side for protection from the wind. Surely we can find some clams or crabs to eat."

"We don't have any way to cook them," Hannah said. "Even if we had flint, everything is too wet."

Dobbs smiled. "I guess we'll eat them raw then."

Hannah shivered and shook her head in an emphatic no. Dobbs shrugged, "Suit yourself."

A mosquito landed on her arm and Hannah slapped at it absentmindedly, distracted by thoughts of a raw meal. Dobbs swatted one near him. "Mosquitoes don't breed in saltwater," he said. "You two set up camp and see what you can find to eat. I'm going to look around a bit for fresh water." He walked back toward the stunted trees and soon disappeared from view. Daniel and Hannah dragged the boat near Ratso. They managed to prop the boat on its side, held up by two heavy pieces of driftwood. The boat would act almost like a roof in case there was more rain. Ratso smiled weakly at them. "I'm not much help. Maybe if I sleep a little I'll feel better."

They gathered some of the tall grasses that grew here and there and piled them to make a bed near the boat. Daniel found two sticks and sharpened them with Ratso's knife. Then, taking the boot to use as a bucket, he and Hannah walked along the shore digging in the sand.

"You look exhausted," Daniel said. His fingers brushed against hers, and for a moment, he held her hand. But just as quickly, he let it go. Hannah looked out over the ocean, peaceful now, gently lapping against the shore. "Standing here, you would never know there was a war.

We could pretend there were no British, or any other bad things. It's like another world."

"Except for the hunger and the mosquitoes," Daniel said, slapping at one briskly. He pointed to a small pool of water that had been trapped during high tide. "Look. Food."

He carefully picked up a small greenish crab and dropped it into the boot.

"Captain Nelson didn't know how helpful his boot was going to be," Daniel laughed. Then, his face fell. His eyes met Hannah's. "I didn't mean to make light of his death," he mumbled.

"I know that," Hannah assured him. "Sometimes it's like that with me too. It doesn't seem real." She helped him gather creatures from the tidal pool. They even discovered two small fish, trapped by the high tide.

When they returned to camp, Dobbs was there tending to Ratso. "There's a swamp not far from here. The water is not salty, but it's not fit to drink either. We'll get some liquid from our dinner," he said, peering into the boot at their catch.

"It will be dark soon. We will eat and rest. As soon as it is daybreak we'd better start walking and see if we can find a village for help."

"What about Ratso?" Hannah asked, when they were far enough away so that the old sailor could not hear.

Dobbs shook his head. "We'll see how he is feeling in the morning. One of us might have to stay behind to care for him."

A few days before, Hannah would not have believed she could ever eat anything raw, but now she watched eagerly as Dobbs dumped out the boot and divided the meal. Using Ratso's knife he cracked open shells and deboned the fish. Hannah gagged at the first bite, but swallowed quickly. "It's not so bad," she said bravely.

The men broke into loud guffaws. "Then why is your face so green?" Daniel teased. Then, to prove they were strong men, Daniel, Ratso, and Dobbs ate their portions with much lip-smacking and pronounced the meal delicious, although Hannah thought Daniel looked a little green himself.

Hannah choked down the rest of her portion. "Even a ship's biscuit would taste good right now," she said. She leaned back against the damaged boat. "It's too bad we couldn't just row further up the island looking for a village."

Dobbs cast a worried look at Ratso. "It would be better," he said. "But the rocks tore a good-sized hole in the bottom and we have no way to fix it."

Daniel sat beside Hannah. It was pleasant, sitting beside him watching the sky darken as purple shadows crept across the dunes. She breathed in the smell of salt and fish and water. The waves, so wild that morning, now gently lapped against the sand.

An orange ball of fur walked out of the rocks and curled up beside them with a satisfied purr. "George!" Hannah cried, delighted to see the old ship's cat. "I wonder what he has been doing."

"Catching a bird dinner, I would guess," Ratso cackled. "George is a survivor."

Hannah picked up the cat and stroked him. "George is a lover," she said as the cat licked her hand.

"George and Mrs. Tibbs could probably live quite comfortably here," Dobbs remarked.

Hannah laid down on the sand and holding George in her arms. "He would miss people, wouldn't you George?" she said as she stroked him.

"After all the fighting he lived through it's a wonder he wants anything to do with people," Daniel observed. "He probably wonders why people are always trying to kill each other. He knows what is really important. A full belly and a good scratching now and then."

The men settled down with groans and finally snores. A full moon rose over the island, lighting the dark like a lantern and leaving a trail of sparkling jewels across the water. Still holding George, Hannah closed her eyes and finally slept.

chapter six

Captured

Hannah opened her eyes at the sound of a gruff voice. "Get up, you dirty rebels!"

Hannah scrambled to her feet. She saw Dobbs and Daniel were struggling to their feet with stunned looks. Six British marines confronted them with muskets at the ready. A British officer watched as one of the marines prodded Ratso with his gun. "Move, rebel, or I'll end your life right here," the officer said coldly.

Daniel moved to help Ratso. But the old man got up, swaying slightly.

"Can't you see he's hurt?" Hannah cried.

The British officer turned to Hannah. He was a handsome man, but his eyes were hard and cruel. "Do you think I care, rebel? I could shoot you all right now and leave your bones for the gulls to pick."

"We sail under a letter of marque from the American government," Dobbs said evenly.

"American government," the officer spat out the words. "As far as I can see you are no better than common pirates. You are all my prisoners." Without another word he strode back to the ship's boat pulled up on the sandy beach. He walked with a swagger.

A sleek frigate was anchored offshore, nearly twice the size of the *Sea Hawk*. One of the marines motioned with his gun, and Hannah, Daniel, Dobbs, and Ratso were forced to march to the ship's boat and climb in.

Several sailors had been left with the boat and they now quickly rowed them to the frigate. The sailors gave them hostile stares and Hannah wondered if they had lost comrades in the fighting. Hannah could not believe they had been captured right when they were so close to freedom. They should have left one person to stand guard, Hannah thought. She guessed by the glum look on Dobbs's face he was thinking the same thing, and probably blaming himself.

As soon as they were onboard the frigate they were pushed and prodded through a hatchway and into a small hold guarded by several marines. The British showed no mercy toward Ratso, pale and sweaty from his injuries and fever. The old man was staggering, but with Daniel and Hannah on either side, he managed to keep up.

"Here's your new home, rebels," one of the marines said cruelly as they were shoved into the room.

The only light came from two small barred windows that allowed the guards to watch them. In the dim light, it was difficult to see their fellow prisoners, but the hold was so full they had to squeeze to find a place to stand. In one corner a wounded man shrieked in agony while others stood helplessly by. The air was foul and stale.

Ratso found a place to sit down with his back against the wall. "At least they didn't search us," Ratso whispered, patting his sash where the coins and small knife were hidden. He then closed his eyes and appeared to sleep.

"Our clothes are so ragged I guess they thought there was no place to hide anything," Daniel said.

Hannah was still stunned by the turn of events. "What's going to happen to us?" she asked Dobbs.

He shrugged. "My guess is that we are headed for one of the prison ships."

"Let's tell the guards Hannah is a girl," Daniel whispered, so Ratso couldn't hear.

Hannah shook her head. "We are in this together."

"Won't do any good anyway. The British will hang a woman just as easy as a man. Not that I think they will hang us," Dobbs added quickly, seeing their alarmed looks. "But I don't think they would hesitate throwing her in prison. If some of these men knew she was a woman, she wouldn't be safe."

Hannah's eyes had adjusted to the low light. She looked around at the other prisoners. Some looked just as lost and afraid as she felt. Others looked hard and merciless. "He's right," she whispered.

"I saw the British hang a nine-year-old girl for stealing bread," Dobbs said. "They think of us as rebellious children."

"I wouldn't put my children in prison," Daniel said bitterly.

"You might if you were a British soldier," Dobbs replied.

The screams from the wounded man had stopped, although he still thrashed about, groaning loudly. Dobbs went over to help. He was back in a minute, shaking his head. "He has terrible burns over most of his body. No one could save him, even with a medicine kit."

When she had first climbed the ropes aboard, Hannah had recognized John Meyer, one of the sailors who had encouraged her on the *Majestic*. Although he was a taciturn man and had seldom spoken to Hannah or Daniel, he greeted them like long-lost friends. "I was afraid everyone from the *Sea Hawk* was dead," he said.

"No," Hannah assured him. "Dobbs is here, and Daniel. Ratso too, although he is wounded."

John Meyer greeted the others. "Was the *Majestic* sunk?" Dobbs asked.

"The British have her back," Meyer said. "Mr. Hailey was not very convincing trying to bluff his way clear, and then got excited and ordered the guns fired. We didn't have enough lads to man all the guns and Mr. Hailey let the British get close enough to board. First, though, they peppered us with grapeshot. Almost everyone was on deck, so most of the men were killed or wounded. Weren't enough men to fight them off. The British boarded the ship and took it back. Later they transferred me to this ship. I don't know what happened to the others."

"Was Jonesy among those killed?" Hannah asked.

Meyer looked at her and then cast his gaze downward. "Aye. He was."

Hannah held back tears as she was reminded again of all the misery they had suffered at the hands of the British.

The guards opened the door and a portly man wearing a crisp captain's uniform stepped into the hold. "I am Captain Rushford. You rebels are prisoners of His Majesty, King George. You will be taken to New York. However, the king is merciful. Any man who would serve in his navy will be pardoned."

No one stepped forward. After a minute the Captain shrugged. "You may change your mind after a time in prison." He stepped back out and slammed the door.

Through the cracks, Hannah could see the guards once again take their places watching the door.

It was quiet for a minute. Then out of the dark a voice spoke. "If any of you think to take the good captain up on his offer, think again. No prison could be worse than serving on a British ship."

The silence returned following the man's speech. Hannah squeezed her way back to Ratso and sat down beside him. "How are you feeling?" she asked.

The old man shook his head. "Not so good. I am thinking I'm not going to make it."

"You have to make it. You are going to help Daniel and me on the farm, remember? And what about those rich old widows, just waiting to meet you?"

In the dim light Hannah could hardly see his face, but she thought Ratso was smiling. "I'll try," he said weakly. "I never like to disappoint the ladies, lad."

Hannah looked down at the old sailor, who looked so small and weak. A small part of her felt like he did not have much time. Although she held out hope for him, she felt there was something she had to tell him.

"Speaking of ladies," Hannah knelt down and whispered in his ear. "Now that we're friends, I should tell you that I am not a lad, but a lady myself."

Ratso's eyes widened as he realized what she had just said. Finally he managed to say, "Well, I'll be. Not a lad, but a lady, he says."

"She says," Hannah whispered with a chuckle. "Can I trust you to keep a secret?"

"I don't know how long I'll last to keep it," he sighed.

"Hush now. Don't say such things." She put her hand gently over his forehead. "My name is Hannah, and I'm glad to be your friend."

Daniel came over and sat beside Hannah. "How is he?" he whispered.

"Not good," Hannah said. "He's burning with fever."

They stayed beside Ratso, talking of the farm, trying to give him reason to fight for life. Hannah told how her father and brother had cleared the trees, using the oxen to pull up the smaller stumps and planting around the ones that were too big. She talked about the evenings when her mother read from the big Bible while her father mended harnesses and the children played checkers, sitting on the floor by the fire. She did not talk about the day the British, Tories, and Indians had come, how they had burned down the house and killed her family.

Late in the afternoon the door was opened again. "Divide yourselves into groups of four," a burly sailor ordered. He handed in pots of food while the marines stood guard. Daniel fetched their pot. It was filled with pease porridge—peas cooked with crumpled ship biscuits—and a small piece of pork. They ate eagerly, even coaxing Ratso to eat some. After the pots and spoons were collected, the marines allowed two prisoners at a time to spend a few minutes on deck. Some of the sailors looked sympathetic, and Hannah wondered if they too were prisoners in a way.

When Hannah's turn came, she breathed deeply, relishing the sun and clean air. All too soon they were escorted back to the hold and two more were allowed on deck. Dobbs helped Ratso, almost carrying him through the hatch. There were several other wounded men, some too seriously injured to make it to the life-giving fresh air, but Ratso had begged to be taken out.

When Dobbs brought Ratso back to the hold, Hannah helped make him as comfortable as she could. Ratso smiled at her. "It is a day to make you glad to be alive," he murmured. He was asleep before Hannah could reply.

"Is there nothing we can do for him anymore?" she asked Dobbs.

Dobbs shook his head. "At least he got some clean air. Captain Rushford is a fair man," Dobbs said. "I doubt we will be treated this well when we get to New York."

They were given no hammocks or blankets for sleeping, and they were packed in so tight that whoever went to the slop bucket stumbled over the sleepers.

Hannah was grateful for the dark when she went to relieve herself. By morning the room reeked of urine and sweaty, unwashed bodies. Two men were allowed to carry the buckets up and dump them into the ocean, but the smell lingered.

Small pots of oatmeal were passed out, along with, surprisingly, cups of watered-down ale. Ratso had not moved, so Hannah shook him gently. “Come on Ratso, you need to eat.” When he still did not move, she shook him again, harder this time. “Ratso, wake up!”

Hearing her distress, Daniel leaned down. He took Hannah’s arm and pulled her up. “He’s gone,” he said. His voice broke.

“Dead?” Hannah cried. “He can’t be.”

Dobbs pushed his way through the crowd of men. He leaned down and felt the old sailor’s head. “At least he died at sea and not rotting in some prison. One of the men with burn wounds died last night too.” He untied the sash around Ratso, and furtively slipped out the knife and two coins. He handed the knife to Daniel and the coins to Hannah. “Hide these well,” he said quietly. Dobbs went to the door and pounded.

“Get back, rebels, before we shoot,” one of the guards yelled.

“We have two dead in here,” Dobbs said.

The door opened and two of the guards tossed in two tattered blankets. Under their watchful eyes, the guards allowed the prisoners to sew the dead men into the blankets for burial. Hannah and Daniel helped lift Ratso onto the blanket and Dobbs sewed.

"You carry the bodies up," one of the guards said as he pointed to four men.

Dobbs stepped forward. "We are his friends," he said quietly. "We should attend to him."

One of the guards seemed about to agree, but another made a menacing motion with his gun. The marine had deep frown lines on his badly pockmarked face. "I don't care if you are his long-lost brother," he growled. "Get back now."

Hannah started to speak, but Dobbs put a hand on her arm. "Pick your battles," he said softly. "Ratso is gone, no matter what we do."

The other dead man's friend made the same objections. "I said, step back!" the guard snarled. Not waiting for the man to comply, the guard gave the man a savage blow on the head with his gun. The prisoner crumpled to the floor, and the guard kicked him. Then the guard looked up. "Any of you other dirty rebels have any objections?"

Daniel's fists were clenched but Dobbs gave a barely perceptible shake of his head. The second guard, looking almost as shocked as the prisoners at the sudden outburst of violence, pointed to the four men who had been chosen. "Pick up the bodies. Be quick about it," he said. The wounded prisoner sat up, holding his head. Suddenly he lurched over to the slop bucket and vomited.

Hannah slid down against the wall. Daniel sat on one side and Dobbs squeezed in on the other as though to give her courage. "We'll make it through this," Daniel said quietly.

Hannah nodded, but in her heart she was not so sure.

chapter seven

Sugar House Prison

Hannah could not believe it had been almost a year since she left Portsmouth, looking for adventure and revenge. Through the tiny windows, she watched as her prison ship docked, dreading what might come next. It was almost autumn now, though the last few days had been hot and humid. The prisoners lived for the few breaths of fresh air when they were allowed on deck. The air in the hold was so foul after weeks at sea that everyone was sick. Even though Captain Rushford gave them food that was not much worse than his crew's, there were days when Hannah could hardly choke it down.

The rats had grown bolder, sometimes running across her while she slept, and she itched constantly from fleabites. Still, she was grateful for the company of Dobbs and especially Daniel. Dobbs entertained them with stories about his long years at sea, the exotic lands he had seen, and the captains he had served. "Captain Nelson was one of the best," he declared.

The prisoners could hear the activity above them and the rasp of chains as the anchor was lowered and the ship shuddered to a stop.

"Well, men," John Meyer said slowly. "Now we find out our fate. I'll wager these past few weeks will seem like a picnic compared to what is next."

"No need to fret before a thing happens," Dobbs said evenly. Hannah could tell from his face that he believed John Meyer was right.

Almost immediately the door swung open. "Out, rebels!" shouted a harsh voice. The prisoners were lined up, carefully watched by marines with their guns ready.

"Stay close," Daniel whispered. "Don't let them separate us."

One of the marines poked Daniel with the muzzle of his gun. "Quiet, rebels! You speak only when told to speak."

The prisoners were marched up to the forecastle deck. Several longboats had already been lowered and were manned by even more marines. The prisoners climbed down the rope ladders and into the waiting boats.

Hannah looked at Daniel. He had lost weight, so that his clothes, little more than rags, hung on him. The beard he had been so proud of growing was longer now, but dirty and snarled. He was unnaturally pale from the hours locked in the dark hold. The prisoners were ordered to row the boats to a small dock. Once there, they were ordered to march through several busy streets. Hannah saw from the signs that they were in New York. They passed a swampy area near some workshops. The people they passed—prosperous-looking merchants, with clean hands and powdered wigs, and ladies who held up their long skirts to avoid the filth of the street—stared at them with unreadable faces and would not meet their eyes. Walking among them were scores of British soldiers.

At last they arrived at a sugar-refining factory built of dark stone, five stories high, with tiny windows. A high fence surrounded it. Inside the gate a wide path circled the building, which was patrolled by guards. At every window faces crowded against the small, barred openings, watching. The marines marched the prisoners into a large room and were made to stand and wait, even though the room was unbearably hot and they were all weak from hunger.

A short man came in carrying a ledger. He stared at them in disgust without speaking. "Any of you that want to redeem yourselves by serving in His Majesty's navy step forward," he said at last. When no one moved he smiled without a bit of warmth. "Well, rebels, let's see if time in my cage will change your mind."

At the man's order, the prisoners stepped forward one by one to state their name, age, and ship.

"Jack Pritchard, fourteen," Hannah said, remembering to make her voice sound low. "I was the cabin boy on the *Sea Hawk*."

"You are young, boy. You could still have a life in the Royal Navy."

"No," Hannah said bitterly. "I'll not serve England."

The man shrugged. "Suit yourself."

As soon as everyone's name had been written in the ledger, the guards prodded them up three flights of stairs and into a room already so crowded with men there was hardly room to squeeze in. The room was long and narrow with only two small windows to let in air. Men crowded around the windows, beating back others who jostled for a position closer to the only source of air. Dobbs struck up a conversation with a man standing near.

"What happens now?" he asked.

The man shook his head. "I've been here for three months."

"Were you on a ship?" Hannah asked.

"No. I was a tailor. After the British captured New York, the Tories came back. They were quick to point out anyone who had helped the cause of freedom. I sewed uniforms."

"And for that they threw you in prison?" Daniel asked.

"There are some here who did nothing, but the Tories, their former friends and neighbors, pointed them out as being patriots. I was told there are more than five thousand of us. At the rate we are dying I suppose the numbers will go down. That is probably why General Howe lets Cunningham get away with what he does."

Seeing their puzzled looks the man explained. "The one who wrote all of your names in his ledger—that's Cunningham. The British supply us prisoners with food. Cunningham sells it and feeds us rotten meat and wormy biscuits. He's getting rich while we die."

As they spoke the people in the room had shuffled slightly and now a new group was able to draw a few breaths of air.

"Has anyone ever escaped?" Daniel whispered.

The man shook his head. "Not a chance. Everything is too well guarded. At any rate you will be too busy just trying to stay alive."

John Meyer pushed his way to them. "There is water in the corner," he said, "although it is slimy and dirty. Better drink it because I have learned that we may not be fed today. They feed us in groups of six. They won't get to everyone today. The British like things done nice and orderly, even their murder."

Without any visible signal, the men in the room milled about so that every few minutes a new group had a few minutes at the windows. Hannah found herself pushed to the center of the room. She stayed close to Daniel, but they did not speak because it took every bit of energy just to breathe. Gradually they were pushed to the outside circle and at last their turn came at the window. Even then there was no great relief. The air outside was hot and steamy. There was only time for a few deep breaths and they were prodded away.

In one corner, there was a barrel of water and a ladle. The men drank as they arrived at that spot. Hannah grabbed the ladle eagerly, only to find the water was slimy and warm. There was a thick layer of sediment in the bottom of the barrel and the water was muddy.

There was a look of despair on Daniel's face that she knew was mirrored on her own. How long could a person stand this without collapsing? And yet she knew some of these men had been here for months.

Now and then a man would pick up a pail, stacked by the door. The guards would let him pass. When he returned a short time later, six men would crouch around the bucket and eat, and another man would be allowed to leave. The food smelled rancid, but Hannah's stomach growled in protest as the crowd pushed her away from even the smell of food.

That night they were forced to sleep on the bare, dirty floor so tightly packed together that there was only room to lie on one side. Occasionally a voice would call out "right" or "left" and every man turned as if one. Hannah had waited for hours to relieve herself. Under cover of night, she made her way to the slop bucket tripping over bodies and being rewarded with grunts and curses.

On the third night, the guards called out three names. Two of the men left their spots stoically, but the third begged and pleaded: "Not me. I've a wife and seven children." The guards beat him unmercifully and dragged him away with the others. The men left behind cursed and swore, making such a ruckus that several guards came and threatened them all. "Quiet, you dirty rebels, or you'll be next to go."

"What's going to happen to those men?" Hannah asked quietly.

"Don't know for sure," the man nearest her whispered. "They never come back. We think they're being hanged."

Hannah was scrunched up against Daniel's back. "Did you hear what he said?" she whispered.

Daniel nodded. "There is nothing we can do."

"What if they decide to hang us?" Hannah whispered. "They could say we were pirates. Pirates are always hanged."

Daniel managed to roll over so that he was facing her. Carefully, making sure no one could see, he took her hand and held it. A tiny shaft of moonlight gleamed in his eyes.

"They won't. We are just more rebels to them," he whispered. "We will find some way to escape. Now get some sleep. We need to save every bit of strength we have for that day."

In the morning a man handed them a small bowl of oatmeal. The man had obviously been fat at one time, but now his skin hung with empty wrinkles. "The ones who were taken last night won't be needing their share," he said grimly. "There's vermin in the oatmeal, but it will keep you going."

"Thank you," Hannah said. She knew the man could have eaten the extra portion and no one would have thought less of him. As if he understood what she was thinking, the man said, "Just because the British treat us like animals, doesn't mean we have to act like animals."

She shared with Daniel and Dobbs. Divided among three there was barely enough to take the edge off her hunger, and she wondered when they would eat again.

The room was even hotter than the day before and the prisoners started their listless shuffle around the room as soon as they had eaten. Sometime in the midmorning the door was thrown open. Cunningham entered the room flanked by two armed guards. He held a large basket, covered with a clean linen cloth. Hunger had sharpened Hannah's senses. Even across the room she could smell the heady scent of fresh-baked bread.

"Silas Procter," Cunningham called. "Step forward."

A thick pall of hate and fear settled over the prisoners. "Cunningham," a prisoner near Hannah spat. "Tis the devil's spawn."

Silas Proctor, dressed in rags, stepped forward as ordered. Although emaciated and barely able to stand, his eyes blazed with defiance.

"Your wife and child came to see me," Cunningham taunted. "Lovely lady. Perhaps she would like some company some evening."

Silas Procter stood silent, his hands clenched into fists. "No? From the looks of you she will soon be a widow lady," Cunningham smiled, lifting the basket cloth and reaching in. "She brought you a present. Looks like honey cakes. Oh, and there is butter and preserves, and boiled eggs. And an orange! Where do you suppose she got that?"

He looked at the grinning guards. "One of your duties is to keep the prisoners safe, is it not? What if the dear lady was anxious for the freedom of widowhood? Possibly this food has been tainted with some kind of poison. As protectors of these prisoners we simply cannot let that happen. We will have to taste all this food to make sure it is safe."

With that he cut large chunks of bread and spread them with the butter and jam, passing pieces to each of the guards.

"Hmm, seems alright," he said with his mouth full. "It is quite delicious, in fact. Your wife is an excellent cook." He slowly peeled the orange, again dividing it. Then he looked in the basket. "Oh dear, there doesn't seem to be anything left. But don't worry. I will tell your wife you thoroughly enjoyed your little picnic." He tossed the empty basket on the floor and with a final chuckle left the room.

Silas Procter slumped weakly against his friends. He stayed curled up all day and the next morning he did not get up. Dobbs bent over him. "Get up. Get angry. Don't let Cunningham win," he said. The hapless man sat up and nodded, but three days later he was dead.

Most of the guards were as cruel as Cunningham, relishing the prisoner's misery and adding to it with taunts and blows for minor infractions. But occasionally, when Cunningham was away at another of the several other prisons he ran, a guard would actually deliver a basket. The same man who had given her the oatmeal that first day gave Hannah a small spoonful of strawberry preserves.

Hannah held the sweet taste of strawberries in her mouth, letting it melt slowly down her throat. The daily rations were barely enough to survive on and often so putrid Hannah could not force herself to choke them down. There were maggots in the meat sometimes and always weevils cooked in the oatmeal. There were never any vegetables or fruit.

Hannah found it harder to get up every morning and join the sad rotation around the room. "You have to stay angry," Dobbs said, repeating what he had told Silas Procter. But Hannah's despair was so great she could not summon the energy to stay angry. Daniel sat beside her, giving up his turn at the small windows. He talked of what life would be like after the war, asking endless questions about her family's farm. One day she told him about the berries that ripened in the woods and the wonderful pies her mother had made.

"It is too bad you could not bake such a pie," Daniel said sadly.

"I can," Hannah told him. "Almost as good as my mother. And I make bread and cake."

Daniel smiled. "How lucky am I. To have a wife who can wield a sword and pistol and bake a pie."

Hannah smiled back. "Who said I was going to be your wife?"

Daniel smiled. "Who else would marry an old pirate woman like you?"

Hannah watched him when he was not looking. She had come to depend on Daniel's quiet strength. In truth, she realized, she could no longer imagine a life without him.

chapter eight

The Prison Ships

Hannah, Dobbs, and Daniel had been in the prison three weeks when their names were called. Hannah stepped forward, her stomach quaking with fear. Were they to be hanged after all?

The guards heaped abuse on them. "Move, you filthy rebels," they shouted, prodding them with guns. They were taken outside, and in spite of her certainty that these would be her last minutes on earth, Hannah breathed deeply, happy to feel a small breeze across her face and to see the blue sky above her. John Meyer was with them, and as they stood waiting, several other small groups joined them until there were nearly fifty men.

The guards forced them to walk through the city, quiet now before the shops were open, and past a mill close to a river. As they approached a small dock and several waiting longboats, Hannah realized that they were not to be hanged this day after all. Dobbs gave a sigh of relief and she knew she was not the only one who had feared for their lives. The land near the dock was swampy and Hannah swatted at the mosquitoes that landed on her face, legs, and neck.

About one hundred yards from the shore there was an old derelict ship anchored in the swift current. There were several other ships in sight but they all seemed to be little more than rotted hulks. With his cutlass drawn, one of the soldiers ordered them into the longboats. "Pick up the oars, rebels. You can row yourselves to your new cage," he said.

"Look carefully," Daniel whispered. "If we escape, we will need to remember where to go."

"The banks are high," Hannah said quietly.

"No talking rebels," one of the guards shouted.

Hannah looked furtively around as they were rowed to the ship. The land around the dock was marshy with a small sandy area along the water. A deep ravine cut through the marsh, becoming thickly forested away from the water. Through the trees she could see a few houses and barns. She nodded to Daniel to show him she had done as he asked, but what she had seen did not encourage her. She was a good swimmer, but the river would be a difficult swim with its swift current. Except for the dock area, the banks seemed too difficult to climb.

As the boats neared the ship, Hannah could see hands waving from the small barred windows. She thought at first they were waving a greeting, but as the boats rowed to the side, she realized the prisoners on the ship were waving them away. "Try to escape and let them shoot you," one man shouted. "It would be a kinder fate than to set foot on this ship."

Truly frightened now, Hannah looked at Daniel. Could this be worse than what they had just endured? The guards ordered the prisoners up the rope ladder. A tent on the forecastle deck offered shade for the many guards. A few prisoners were out in the sun scrubbing the deck under a guard's watchful eyes.

Hannah and the other new prisoners were led to a small ship's store below deck, and each man was issued a blanket and a hammock. "Keep watch on your blanket," the purser said. "Winter is not far off. And you will not be issued another. You can buy these if you have money," he said, motioning to the shelves that contained small sacks of tobacco and coffee, a few articles of clothing, and extra blankets.

From the ship's store, the guards led the prisoners to the "tween" deck area. "Welcome to your new home, rebels," the head guard said with a sneer.

Hannah's horror grew as she looked around the long low-ceilinged room. While not quite as crowded as the town prison, the smell of sickness and death hung over the gaunt men who greeted them with dull eyes. Most of the hammocks had been rolled up and hung on the wall, although some men still occupied theirs, groaning with sickness. At one end, several crates had been arranged into a table and chairs. Several prisoners sat there listlessly playing cards, but for the most part the men just sat on the floor. A large rat ran boldly across the room. The vermin finally disappeared into a hole in the wall. But no one looked alarmed or tried to kill it.

"What sickness have you?" Dobbs asked, pointing to the occupied hammocks.

One of the healthier prisoners shrugged. "Yellow fever, dysentery, smallpox."

Dobbs looked alarmed. "Smallpox?"

The prisoner pointed to three men still in their hammocks at the end of the room. "We've tried to stay away from them except to bring them water. I think we are safe. It has been ten days and no one else has sickened."

Dobbs still looked worried. "It takes twelve days. You could all be sick in the next few days. I have had smallpox," he said to Daniel and Hannah pointing to the scars on his face.

Daniel nodded. "I had it when I was a young. It killed my parents, but hardly touched me." He showed them several pockmarks on his arm.

Hannah shook her head. "I've never had it."

Dobbs thought for a minute. "Once when I was sailing off the coast of Africa I was told about a protection. It is called variolation. What you do is give yourself a small dose of the sickness. As weak and hungry as we all are Jack, you will surely get it. If you do, the chances are great that you will not survive in the filth and squalor of this ship. I don't know that this will work, but at least it will give you a fighting chance."

Hannah nodded. "I trust you."

Dobbs furtively held out his hand to Daniel. "Do you have Ratso's knife?"

Daniel discreetly worked the knife out of his sash and handed it to Dobbs, who walked over to the sick men. He inspected their pox sores, and spoke to one of them. When the man nodded, Dobbs took the knife and scraped off one of the sores.

"Give me your hand," Dobbs said when he returned.

Daniel stepped forward. "Are you sure about this Dobbs? Maybe if Jack stays away from the sick men he will be all right."

"If I am right, most of these men will be sick in a few days. There is no way Jack would escape," Dobbs said quietly. He turned to Hannah. "It is your choice. You will get smallpox this way, but it will likely be less severe. Since Daniel and I have both had it, we can care for you."

Hannah held out her hand. She flinched as Dobbs made a small cut between her fingers and thumb. Then he cut off the bottom of his shirt and wrapped it around her wounded hand.

"What about the other prisoners?" Hannah asked.

Dobbs shook his head. "I think it's too late for them."

When the prisoners ate that evening, there was no food for the newcomers. "They will give you food tomorrow," one of the men said. "If you can call the garbage Cunningham buys for us food."

"Why does he hate us so much?" Hannah asked one of the prisoners.

"I heard that Cunningham was the leader of a gang of bully boys that liked to beat up patriots. One day, the Sons of Liberty caught him. They made him get on his knees and shout for liberty. He's never forgotten that humiliation, and he found the perfect revenge."

"Do you think General Howe knows what he's doing?" Dobbs asked.

"How could he not know?" the man said bitterly. "Cunningham was the scum of the earth. Why give him a high-paying job unless you were hoping he could make us all disappear."

"Are there ever prisoner exchanges?" Daniel asked.

"Few," the man said. "Usually army officers. Never privateers. A few families have managed to bribe their loved ones free, but not many."

"How about escaping? Has anyone managed that?" Daniel asked.

The man looked at him a long time as though trying to decide if they could be trusted. "A few of us are trying," he said. "The wood is rotten. We are cutting through the side. Each day we replace the loose boards. We have to be careful because the guards make regular rounds."

"I'll help," Daniel said quietly.

"So will I," Hannah said.

The man nodded. "I'm Samuel Stewart," he said, offering his hand. "I was a printer before this. The English didn't like my editorials."

Late that night Hannah heard Daniel whispering to Dobbs. "I think it's foolhardy," Dobbs said. "That many men trying to escape at once. The English are no fools. They are bound to find out."

"Would you rather sit here and starve?" Daniel whispered fiercely.

Dobbs was silent for a minute. Aware that others could hear him, he said, "What about Jack? He's going to need care when he gets sick."

"I thought that thing you did would keep him from getting sick," Daniel said. Hannah could feel Daniel looking at her although she kept her eyes closed and pretended to sleep.

"He will get sick," Dobbs said. "Hopefully it will be a light case."

"Hopefully?" Daniel sounded angry. "You don't really know?"

"Look at him. He is thin and weak. This is his only chance. Go if you must but don't take Jack. I'm not much of a swimmer anyway, so I will stay and care for him."

"I can't leave without Jack," Daniel said, his voice tortured with indecision. "He is my friend."

Hannah opened her eyes. "You go. When you get to Portsmouth, if you can't find Mr. Gaines, make your way to an Inn called the Red Rooster. My friends Lottie and Madeline may help you buy us out of here. We can pay them back out of the treasure."

Daniel still looked troubled. "I don't want to leave you . . . two. I will have to think on it."

Hannah found it impossible to sleep. Her stomach growled with hunger and her hand hurt where Dobbs had cut it. The hatches had been sealed shut and although there was some air from the tiny windows, the room was stuffy and hot. The sick men groaned, begging for help, and some of the others cried out and cursed in their sleep. Several of the sickest men were delirious, thrashing about and screaming. In the morning Hannah could hardly move in her hammock. Dobbs unwrapped her bandage and examined her already festering hand. "I think it has taken," he said grimly. "All we can do now is hope."

As soon as they roused, the guard shouted, "Bring up your dead, rebels."

Three men had died during the night. Other prisoners carried them up to the deck. The guards, joking and talking among themselves as if they were handling bundles of cargo, lowered the bodies by ropes into the longboats. The prisoners remained silent, although their eyes burned with hate at the guards' indifference. Several prisoners were chosen to handle the burial. While the bodies were rowed to shore, the guards ordered the rest of the prisoners to roll up their bedding and carry it to the deck. They were allowed to have a good drink from the water barrel. Surprisingly, the water was fairly fresh and Hannah drank deeply. Afterward they scrubbed the deck under the watchful eyes of the guards. While she scrubbed the deck, Hannah watched the boat carrying the dead prisoners. At the dock, the prisoners dumped the bodies into a wheelbarrow and pushed them to a sandy strip near the beach. Shallow graves were dug and the prisoners dumped the bodies and covered them. The prisoners rowed back to the ship, while the guards watched, laughing.

The prisoners were allowed to stay on deck and although the sun beat down on them unmercifully, it was better than being confined below. Hannah wondered what it would be like in winter with only one thin blanket for protection.

The rebels who had been prisoners for months were emaciated and ragged, but the Spanish and French prisoners looked scarcely human. They were quartered deep in the dark holds and fed even worse than the Americans, with little more than moldy biscuits and rancid oil. Most could scarcely walk, they were so weak, and had been forced to carry up their own dead, which added five to the pile of bodies.

At midmorning, Dobbs's name was called and he was allowed to go to a window where he was given the dinner ration for himself, Hannah, Daniel, John Meyer, and another newcomer called Shorty. He then took the rations—slightly spoiled meat, more moldy biscuits, and a few peas—to the galley to be boiled. It was an unappetizing mess, but Hannah was so ravenous that she treated it like it a feast.

"We are fortunate to get it cooked," John Meyer remarked between bites. "Some of them had to eat their rations raw the first day. I can't stand this treatment. I was a respectable clock maker before all this happened."

After they ate, Daniel sought out Samuel Stewart, who was sitting on a crate smoking a long-stemmed pipe.

"Wouldn't this be a good time to be working while the guards are all occupied watching up here?"

"Patience, my young friend," Samuel answered. "It would arouse immediate suspicion if we were to go below rather than stay up here in the fresh air."

Embarrassed at the chiding, Daniel stood at the rail looking glumly at the shore, so near and yet so far. Hannah said nothing, lost in her own thoughts. She was afraid for Daniel to join the ones who planned an escape, yet she knew it might be their only chance. And though she tried to put the coming sickness out of her mind, she could not. Two of the dead men that very morning had died of smallpox, and their bodies had been covered with festering sores just like the ones forming on Hannah's hand.

That night after the hatchways were locked, Daniel and Hannah joined a group of prisoners below deck. Faint light from the moon's reflection on the heavy clouds barely penetrated the tiny windows, and the men had to work by feel, chipping at the wood and carefully sweeping up any stray chips. With the addition of Ratso's knife to the meager collection of tools, the work went more quickly, until one of the men tripped, dropping the knife and staggering into the hull with a loud thump. The men froze, but the sound of boots hurrying down the hatch steps propelled them into action. Hannah dived for her hammock. Daniel scooped up the knife before he too flipped into his hammock and closed his eyes. By the time two guards barged in carrying a lantern, everyone was seemingly asleep.

The guards looked about suspiciously. Hannah held her breath. In the light from the guard's lantern she could see a fresh gash in the wood—there had been no time to fix the piece back in place. The guards walked slowly around the room. In a minute they would see the damaged wood. With little time to think, Hannah stuck her finger in her throat. She retched loudly, and leaped from her hammock and ran to the slop bucket. She knelt in front of the damaged wood, obscuring it from the guards' view.

The guards laughed. "Our food doesn't seem to suit the rebel lad," one of them joked.

Once started, the contents of her stomach continued to come up. Over and over she retched, until there was nothing left. Even then the terrible smell of the bucket gave her the dry heaves. Still laughing, the guards kept walking.

Wiping her mouth on her sleeve, Hannah stumbled back to her hammock. The guards finished their inspection and, seeming to be satisfied, left. A few seconds later the hatchway was closed and Hannah heard the sound of the sliding bolt locking them in.

"Are you sick, Jack?" Samuel Stewart called out.

"The lad saved us from a whipping, or worse," another man whispered. "The guards would have seen our work for sure if he had not acted."

"Good lad," Samuel Stewart whispered. "We had best leave off our work for a few days, since we've raised the interest of the guards."

Several men groaned, but eventually agreed that it was better to curtail the work for a few days. It was a wise decision because twice more that night—and for several nights thereafter—the guards would burst in for random inspections.

The days fell into a terrible routine of wretched food and mind-numbing hours with nothing to do. Every day more men were brought to the ship, balanced by the number of prisoners who died. Hannah quickly learned which guards to avoid. There were some who relished in their power, beating and cursing the prisoners for the slightest offense. Others were watchful, but seldom mistreated the prisoners. The German-speaking Hessian guards, hired by the British, were even somewhat friendly.

One day Hannah noticed men milling about, talking in hushed but excited tones. Usually despondent, or at best angry, she was surprised to see some of the men actually smile.

"What's happening?" she asked Samuel Stewart. "Has someone had good news of the war?"

"Wish that it were," Samuel said with a shake of his head. He pointed to a small boat rowed by an old plump woman approaching the prison ship. "Who is that?" Hannah asked.

"She has things to sell. Fruit, vegetables, and bread. If you have money," he explained further. "Some of the families are able to bribe the guards into delivering packages. That one there, Benedict Tourney, always manages to get his packages delivered." He pointed out a sharp-faced man who had pushed his way to the head of the line.

Several of the men haggled with the woman. Daniel, Hannah, and Dobbs huddled together. "We could use one of Ratso's doubloons," Dobbs suggested. "It is worth more than the small coins the others have. Shall we trust her to give us the proper amounts back?"

"There is another problem," Daniel said. "Only a few of the men have money. The others are desperate. If they realize we have doubloons, we may be robbed."

"I don't think we have any choice. We have to trust her. If we are questioned we could say that it was a lucky piece, and the only one we possess," Hannah suggested.

They agreed that Dobbs would be the one to negotiate. "See if she can bring us paper and post a letter," Hannah suggested. "If I could get a letter to Lottie and Madeline, they may try to buy our freedom. Maybe they can find

Mr. Gaines and he would give them our share from the first ship."

The guards, keeping out of the hot sun under their canvas tent, paid scant attention to the haggling. Evidently they knew the old woman and trusted her not to smuggle weapons to the men. The food was bundled up so that it could not be seen and this made her even more suspicious. The other men seemed familiar with her, though, and the ones with a few coins passed them to her. Balancing in her tiny boat, she handed up the bundles through the rail. Dobbs still looked doubtful, but he leaned over the rail to talk to the woman. Finally he handed her one of the doubloons. The old woman looked at it carefully. "What do you want for it?" she asked.

"Paper and writing pen and ink and your promise to post the letter. Plus three bundles of food each of the next five times you come," Dobbs said.

"Three bundles, three times," she countered.

"Four," Dobbs said. "And a warm blanket."

"You drive a hard bargain," the old woman cackled, handing up three bundles. "I will bring the writing supplies next week."

chapter nine

Betrayal

Although Dobbs was not convinced the old woman would keep her promise, Hannah remained hopeful. She looked for a bright spot in the misery and despair surrounding them. "At least she brought good food for our money," she said. "Although I wish it had lasted longer."

The old woman's bundles had been filled with fresh apples, bread, jam, small packets of coffee and sugar, butter, and a few carrots and onions. They each had hoped to make their food supply last until the old woman returned, but it had been impossible to hoard their bounty while their fellow prisoners starved.

Spread among so many, there had only been a few bites for each. But Hannah comforted herself with the belief that she may have helped some live a few days longer. Even the few other prisoners who had the means to buy the old woman's bundles had been shamed into sharing. The exception was Benedict Tourney, who kept mostly to himself and had managed to stay soft and plump while those around him starved.

"Have you no shame?" Samuel Stewart said, motioning toward Hannah. "Even this poor lad has shared his bounty."

"I am not responsible for the rest of you. If those fools want to give away their supplies, let them. It will be just that much sooner that they are carried up with the dead. I intend to live, and the devil can take the rest of you." Benedict took his bundle into his hammock, carefully cradling it in his arms as he slept. In the morning, as soon as the guards made their grim demand for the dead to be brought up, Hannah saw him frantically searching around his hammock, cursing loudly when he realized his hoard was missing.

"What seems to be the problem?" Shorty asked.

"My food is missing. As if you didn't know," Benedict shouted, glaring angrily around the room. "Which one of you did this?"

"Maybe you ate it in your sleep," Samuel Stewart offered.

"Somebody will pay for this when I find out who did it," Benedict swore, his voice shaking with helpless fury.

The men, who had gathered around to watch, chuckled, and walked away, leaving him alone with his fiery rage.

In spite of the fresh food, the death toll continued to climb by the day. Nearly twenty men had smallpox. Although they were quarantined at one end of the room, their suffering was terrible to see and hear. Every morning the guards opened the hatch and called, “Bring up your dead, rebels,” and sometimes there were seven or eight men to be buried in the shallow graves along the shore. Still, the ship was crowded because every day more prisoners arrived. Most were privateers captured by the British warships.

The stifling heat of summer had given way to warm days and cool, crisp nights that signaled the beginning of autumn. “We’re going tomorrow night,” Daniel whispered. “If we wait any longer the water will be too cold to swim in.”

Hannah’s heart pounded with anticipation and fear. “I’ll go with you,” she said. “It has been fourteen days and I’m still not sick.”

“Can you swim that far?” Daniel asked quietly.

“I’m a good swimmer,” Hannah said. “I used to swim in the river with my brother.”

“I’ll talk to the men,” Daniel said. “There are only six of us going.”

The next morning Hannah awoke with a severe headache and a sore neck. Dobbs felt her head. "I probably just slept in a bad position," she protested.

Dobbs shook his head. "No lad, I think it is starting."

"Not now. We are supposed to escape tonight," Daniel groaned. He laid his hand on Hannah's head, and looked at Dobbs. "He's burning with fever. Can't you do something?"

"Find a rag and soak it. It may soothe him. And find him something to eat before he gets worse," Dobbs said.

The call came for the dead to be carried up. Men carried a body past Hannah. Although wrapped, the blanket had fallen back as he was moved and Hannah could see the dead man's face. It was hideously pitted with oozing pus-filled sores. She shuddered. "Is that going to happen to me?" she asked weakly.

"I am hoping you will only get an easy sickness," Dobbs said as he took the wet rag from Daniel and laid it on her head. Although the coolness soothed her, even the touch of the rag made her skin ache.

"Try to sleep," Dobbs said.

Hannah closed her eyes. She heard the shuffle of feet as the men moved to the upper deck. Sometime in the morning she heard a joyful cry. The old woman was back. "I guess we will find out if she has kept her word," she heard Dobbs say to Daniel.

"I'll stay with him," Daniel's voice answered. "Don't worry. I'm here. I've decided not to go with the others."

Hannah opened her eyes in spite of the pain that stabbed through her head. "No, you have to go. Find some way to the treasure and buy us out. At least one of us will be free."

"I've thought about it. I am not going without you. We will find a way when you are better," Daniel said stubbornly, glancing back at the door. "Dobbs is back. It looks like she brought the food. If the woman remembered the paper we can write to your friends. Maybe they can help us."

Dobbs dropped the bundles on the floor. "She will wait if we can write this letter quickly. She brought paper, a quill, and ink."

Hannah struggled to sit up, but the fever had already made her too weak. She sank back down and closed her eyes. "You write it. Send it to Lottie and Madeline at the Red Rooster Inn on Queens Street in Portsmouth."

Dobbs took the quill and dipped it in the ink. Using a crate for a table he wrote swiftly, the quill scratching across the page. "We can't tell them about the treasure. The wrong person may read it. I've told them that even if they can't find Mr. Gaines we have the means to pay them the money back."

"Send them my love," Hannah said softly. "And tell them I am sorry I ran off without telling them."

"We have no way to seal it," Dobbs said. "The old woman promises she will send it to Boston with someone she knows. From there it can go on a stagecoach with the regular post." He hurried out to give the letter to the old woman.

Daniel opened the food bundles. Although there did not seem to be as much food as the first time, what was there was fresh and good. He buttered a piece of bread and coaxed Hannah into swallowing a few bites.

Once again, they shared some of their food with other starving prisoners who could not afford to buy their own. Once again, Benedict Tourney hoarded his, ignoring the angry curses.

Dobbs insisted on saving some food for Hannah, but she shook her head weakly when urged to eat.

A few hours after the hatches had been locked, Hannah heard Samuel Stewart speak to Dobbs and Daniel. "We are going now. Good luck to you and the lad there. Are you sure you will not come with us?" he asked Daniel.

"I can't leave my friend Jack," Daniel said. "I would be no better than Tourney."

The men lined up. Samuel carefully removed the wood, leaving a hole wide enough for one man at a time to slip through. The prisoners who were not trying to escape gathered around, whispering goodbyes. Hannah noticed Benedict Tourney standing alone, watching silently. She could see his face in the dim light from the moon. Something about the way he watched so intently made her uneasy and she called quietly to Daniel. "I have a bad feeling about this," she said, but before she could explain, a volley of shots rang out, and then another and another. The sixth man, who was just about to slip out into the water, pulled himself back in, gasping in terror. "They were waiting for them. The guards are in the longboats almost like they knew we were going tonight. It was a trap."

Hannah looked at Benedict Tourney. In the moonlight his eyes glittered with malevolence. Daniel was still standing by her hammock, his face white. If he had gone with the men as planned, he would have been doomed. "Get Dobbs," Hannah whispered.

Daniel bent down to her. "What is it? Are you worse?"

"Look at Tourney," she said, so quietly only Daniel could hear. "I think he told. He was watching before the men left as though he was waiting for something to happen."

They were interrupted by the sound of marching boots. The door opened and five armed guards burst in, menacing the unarmed prisoners with drawn cutlasses and pistols. Two more guards dragged Samuel Stewart between them.

They dropped the badly bleeding captive on the floor and one of them gave him a vicious kick. "That's what happens when you try to escape, you filthy rebels. The rest of your friends are at the bottom of the river."

"Line up," shouted one of the guards.

"Some of us are sick and dying," Dobbs pleaded.

"You should have thought of that before you tried to escape," the guard answered. "Anyone who doesn't line up will be shot."

Dobbs and Daniel supported Hannah, helping her to her feet. Other men helped their friends until everyone was in line. The guards made them crowd into the far end of the room, leaving their hammocks unused. "You can stay there until the carpenters come to fix the damage," the head guard said, showing no pity to the sick and wounded.

Most of the men had managed to grab their blankets, and they spread them on the dirty floor. The guards who were left in the room glared at them. Samuel Stewart was left alone to slowly bleed to death. Hannah could hear his ragged breath grow faint, and then, with a shuddering sigh, suddenly stop. The only emotion she had left was gratitude that Daniel had not been one of the unfortunate men. She looked around trying to find Benedict Tourney, wondering if he had any shred of remorse. He was sitting up, staring at the guards as if he was trying to get their attention. She was not the only one watching him. Several other prisoners stared at him as they muttered quietly among themselves.

In the morning, two guards fetched Benedict Tourney. He was to be taken to the gunroom where the ship's officers were quartered. Although the officers lived in miserable conditions also, their quarters were not as crowded and most had been allowed to bring a few belongings. If there had been any doubt of Benedict Tourney's guilt, it was gone now. "Say your prayers," Shorty said to Benedict, as he was escorted out. "This will be your last day on earth."

"Did you hear that?" Benedict screamed to the guards. "They threatened me."

"What did you expect," the guard sneered.

"You have to protect me," Benedict begged, almost hysterical now.

"We promised you better quarters," the guard said with indifference. "Not protection."

As the guards led the terrified informer away, Dobbs shook his head. "He wanted to make sure he survived this war, and all he did was ensure that he would not. He will be fortunate to last the day."

chapter ten

Winter

Dobbs's prediction turned out to be true. Although Benedict Tourney was safe enough in the officer's area, as soon as the men assembled on deck, he was killed and his body pushed into the river—all conveniently overlooked by the guards.

"War is a terrible thing," Dobbs said. "In normal circumstances, Mr. Tourney might have been a regular citizen, respected by his friends and family. He might have even given to the poor. Who knows?"

"We're never going to win this war," Hannah said through cracked lips. "There are too many of them and they are too strong."

Daniel nodded in sad agreement, but Dobbs said, "The British soldier fights because that's his job, but we fight for freedom, for ourselves, and for the right to build a great nation like the world has never known. Miracles can happen when you are fighting for a dream."

Daniel had saved a piece of soft bread for Hannah, but it hurt too much to chew. When Dobbs inspected her mouth, he saw two sores, one on her tongue and one on the inside of her cheek. "You are starting to break out," he said. "I know it hurts, but I have seen worse."

Hannah doubted she could feel any worse and still be alive. She was feverish and the rough floor made her body ache more. Her head hurt so bad that even the quiet talk among the men made it worse.

On the third day after the thwarted escape attempt, the British carpenters arrived to repair the hole with long planks of wood. They were soldiers too, but evidently had not served in the prisons before because they looked at the prisoners with horror and pity. They worked quickly, and looked relieved when their work was inspected and approved and they could leave. The repairs covered one of the tiny windows, adding gloom and darkness to the already wretched room. But Daniel saw a bright spot. "With winter coming that will mean less cold air coming in," he remarked.

When the carpenters left, the guards did too, and the prisoners were allowed to move back to their hammocks. Daniel had managed to find an extra blanket, and he tucked it around Hannah. "My legs itch and hurt," she said. Pulling up her pants legs, she gasped at the sight of dozens of festering sores covering her skin.

"Try not to scratch at them," Dobbs said, rubbing on some salve he had gotten from the old woman along with the bundles of food. "You are lucky to only have two spots on your face."

"I don't feel very lucky," Hannah grumbled.

"You must be getting better if you have the strength to be grouchy," Dobbs said.

The next morning, she realized that she did feel slightly better, and although Dobbs warned that she was a long way from well, she managed to eat a few bites of oatmeal. Daniel stayed by her side, cheering her as much as he could, telling her all his dreams for the future.

"How long do you think it will take for the letter to reach Portsmouth?" she asked one day.

Daniel shook his head. "Maybe weeks. And then time to find the money, if they can, and travel here. It may be spring before we hear any news."

Two weeks passed before Hannah was well enough to go up on deck and she was amazed at the difference in the weather. A frigid wind cut through her clothes and made a sharp pain in her chest when she breathed. Dobbs had used another coin and asked the old woman to bring them coats in addition to food for a few more weeks. "I asked her to bring more apples and carrots. They will keep longer if she can't come because of the weather."

Hannah's teeth chattered with another blast of icy wind. "Let's go back down," Daniel said insistently, gently guiding her to the hatch. Below, it was cold and dismal, but at least they were sheltered from the wind. The room was crowded. The longboats had brought twenty more men that very morning.

Hannah and Daniel wrapped themselves in their thin blankets and huddled next to Dobbs on the dirty floor.

"I'm going to talk to the new men to see if they have any information about the war," Dobbs said. Hannah watched him mingle with the newcomers, and frown as he listened to their news.

When Dobbs returned, he looked grim. "Everyone says the war is going badly," he reported. "Some of those men were privateers captured near the Carolinas like we were. They say we have failed to reclaim Savannah from the blasted English."

Tears of despair ran down Hannah's cheeks and she wiped them away furiously. "What is it?" Dobbs said. "Are you sick again?"

Hannah shook her head. "Sometimes I just don't think I can stand any more," she gasped. "I've got lice, and flea bites all over me. I am probably ugly from the pox scars. I just want to . . . "

"Want to what, lad?" Dobbs asked gently.

"Take a bath in rose-scented water," Hannah whispered, laughing between her tears. "I can't wait for the year 1779 to end. It's been one horror after another."

"I have something that might cheer you up," Daniel said suddenly. "I was going to wait until it was all done, but maybe this is a good time. He flipped over one of the crates they used as chairs. The bottom was a carefully painted checkerboard.

"I used the rest of the ink the old woman brought," he explained. "And I am carving the pieces out of a board. I don't have any way to color the pieces, so I am carving an x on some and an o on others."

Hannah smiled. "All this work just so you can get beat," she teased.

"Ha," Daniel grinned. "I have to be careful so the guards don't know I have a knife, but I'll have the pieces finished in a few days. Then we shall see if you can live up to all your big talk."

The next day the old woman brought extra apples, carrots, turnips, and onions. "She said she didn't find coats, but she did bring us extra blankets," Dobbs explained.

"Did you ask her about the letter?" Hannah whispered anxiously.

Dobbs nodded. "She says her friend has not gone to Boston yet. She still promises she will send it."

The next week the old woman did not return, nor the week after that. Finally, one of the kinder guards told them that he heard the woman was dead, carried away by a bad fever.

The winds blew across the ship and one morning the deck was covered in snow. Half of the prisoners had dysentery and a new fever swept through the ship. The death toll rose sharply. Dobbs doled out the little bit of food they had left, but it was not enough to stop the gnawing hunger. The rations were worse, often little more than putrid meat boiled with crumbled ship's biscuits that made a vermin-filled scum. In spite of her hunger, Hannah could not choke it down.

One day a small British supply boat came to bring wood for the guards' fire. The men who brought the wood did not appear to be part of the regular forces. They brought a few apples with them, which they threw out into the crowd of hundreds of desperate, hungry prisoners, laughing and joking at the riots that erupted on deck.

As the ship became packed with prisoners and the winter weather settled in, the guards built a wooden shelter on the deck. Inside the shelter they laid out bricks and sand with a huge metal kettle for a fire, making their duty, if not comfortable, at least tolerable. Except for a few rounds each day and night, the guards stayed in the warmth of their shelter.

Dobbs and Hannah led a contingent to the shelter to beg for some means of making a fire. "We are freezing here," he pleaded. "Some of the men have frostbite on their fingers and toes."

"Should have thought of that before you became a rebel," sneered one of the guards, a Tory. The Tories always seemed the cruelest, perhaps because they had been treated badly by the patriots before New York was taken over by the British.

The captain of the guards stepped forward. "What is the problem?" he asked. His eyes swept over the crowd of prisoners, as though looking for an excuse to inflict new cruelties.

Shorty stepped forward and screamed, "Look at my hands." He held up fingers showing the black and grey of frostbite. "I am a clock maker. How can I resume my trade when this is over with fingers frozen like this?"

The guard captain waved him away, but Shorty stepped closer.

"Back!" the guard shouted, aiming his pistol at Shorty. Dobbs grabbed Shorty, intent on pulling him back, but the clock maker shook him off and took another step forward. There was a sudden blast of gunfire and Shorty stopped, a surprised look on his face. He crumpled to the deck, blood pooling around him, freezing almost instantly into a dark red slush.

Hannah gasped in horror at the man sprawled on the deck. Daniel's arm held her steady. Dobbs stared at the captain. "That was not necessary, Captain," he said gently. "He only wanted you to see his hands."

The captain turned his pistol to Dobbs. "Clean this up," he said coldly. "Or you'll be next."

The mood among the prisoners was utter despair after Shorty's disastrous encounter. But a few days later one of the Hessian guards brought bricks, sand, a metal cauldron, and a bag of coal. The fuel burned smoky, leaving the walls covered with gritty soot. By rotating as they had done in the city prison, however, each man had a few minutes to warm his hands.

Hannah fretted about the letter Dobbs had given the old woman. Had she posted it before she died? Did it fall into the wrong hands? Somehow, not knowing made the waiting even worse.

"It doesn't do any good to worry about it," Daniel told her. "She either posted it or she didn't. Worrying won't change it. Come on, I will give you another chance to beat me at checkers."

The truth was they were evenly matched. Some of the other men played too, using Daniel's crude board. There was little else to pass away the hours, although a few of the men had cards and John Meyer had a Bible that he read out loud in a pleasing melodic voice.

Daniel and Dobbs plotted endlessly, looking for ways to escape. At first the only plan was to wait until spring when the water was warmer, and try to swim ashore. One day, however, Daniel called Hannah to the starboard rail. "Look," he whispered.

Hannah leaned over as far as she could. At first she saw nothing, but then a gust of wind pushed a small boat into view.

"It's just the supply boat, bringing wood for those nasty guards," said Hannah.

"Yes, but . . ." Just then Daniel noticed a guard across the deck staring at them. "I'll tell you later."

That night, Daniel said to her and Dobbs, "I've been watching when the supply boats come. They are manned by regular guards and two guards stay with the boat. The men who bring the wood come and stay for several cups of grog, and to play their cruel game. And all that time the boat is unguarded."

Hannah frowned. She knew what he meant by cruel game, remembering her fellow prisoners clawing at each other to try to get a withered apple.

Dobbs nodded and frowned. "It is indeed an opportunity. The only way to the boat would be to swim around the hull. I am not sure we would survive the icy water. Jack is still weak from the smallpox. In addition to that, we would have to row to shore in the same wet clothes."

The men looked at Hannah. "What do you think?" Daniel asked. "We will not go without you."

Hannah had recovered from the ravages of smallpox, but her body remained frail and weak from lack of food, and even a short excursion to the deck made her tired. She wanted to escape, but she feared her weakness would endanger her friends.

"Let's work on our plans a bit," Dobbs said before she could confess her worries. "First we need a diversion. Something to keep the guards distracted for a few minutes. That water is perilously cold. I think we can survive the few minutes it will take to reach the boat, but not if we continue wearing icy wet clothes. If we had some rope we could lower dry clothes and blankets."

"The fewer clothes we have on to drag us down, the better it will be," Daniel said, excited now that his idea was becoming a reality.

Dobbs nodded, "Something that we can peel off quickly while we are rowing. We still have some doubloons left, so let me see what I can do."

"I'll ask John Meyer if he wants to go with us," Daniel said excitedly.

"I doubt that he will. His family got word to him. They think they can bribe him free," Dobbs said. "He might help with a diversion, however."

Just the thought of escaping their nightmare gave them energy. Hannah choked down the rancid rations, trying to build whatever strength she could.

In the meantime, clothes were wrapped in bundles and enough rope had been found or woven from scraps of cloth to lower them almost to the water's surface. After dark, the day before the wood boat was due to return, Dobbs handed Hannah some rough cloth. Even in the dark she could see his teeth flash in a grin.

"What is it?" she whispered.

Dobbs laughed. "Your swimming outfit. Men's woolen underwear."

Hannah nervously fingered the tattered cloth. It was crusty with who knows what and she could almost feel the vermin crawling through the threads. Stoically, she wiggled into them and put her own clothes on over them.

The next afternoon the wood boat arrived right on schedule. Hannah, Daniel, and Dobbs waited impatiently while the wood was unloaded and stacked on the deck. They could hear the guards inside the shelter stamping their feet, complaining about the cold as they crowded around the fire and poured their first glass of grog. They waited longer, fearing that on this day the guards would not play their cruel game.

"What if they don't do it?" Hannah fretted.

"They will," Daniel said quietly. "They never miss a chance to mistreat us." Even as he spoke an apple sailed into a crowd of prisoners and the guards lined up, taking bets and shouting insults. "Look at them scrabbling around like animals," one guard shouted.

John Meyer had arranged for two of the prisoners to start a huge fight as a distraction, and from the shouts they had kept their word. The guards were taking wagers on the winner. "Now," Dobbs whispered. While the guards were distracted, Hannah, Daniel, and Dobbs edged behind the winch and quickly shed their outer clothes, wrapping them in their blankets. Dobbs tied the bundle and Daniel lowered it over the side. Dobbs had estimated the distance perfectly, the bundles bobbed just above the water. Using the same rope, they slid down. They climbed over the bundle carefully, so as not to loosen it, and slipped into the frigid water.

Hannah gasped in shock. The icy water caused prickles of pain and she was unable to catch her breath. Dobbs had gone first. He was not a good swimmer, and was floundering a bit, but he headed toward the boat determinedly. Hannah heard Daniel behind her. "Go! Go!" he whispered raggedly.

Hannah struck out for the small boat. The pain had stopped and now her body felt numb. She was shaking so hard she could not tell if she was making progress or not, but at last the boat was there. Daniel climbed in first. Dobbs untied the rope, shoved Hannah up with one hand, and climbed in himself. Hannah could not believe the guards had not heard their frantic splashing, but high above she could hear their laughter. It seemed that John Meyer's friends were providing plenty of distracting entertainment. Rowing as silently as they could, they rounded the hull. Daniel reached for the dry clothes and sliced them free with Ratso's knife. Daniel's lips were blue, and his teeth were chattering, like Hannah's, so loud that she was amazed the guards did not hear. Wrapped in blankets, they peeled off the frozen wet clothes and wiggled into dry ones. In spite of being drier now, their bodies still trembled violently as they struck out for shore.

Hannah risked a glance over her shoulder just as a volley of shots rang out from the ship. A musket ball whizzed by her head, narrowly missing.

"Row," Dobbs shouted between his clenched teeth.

Gripping the oars, Hannah rowed with all her strength as round after round was fired at them. A tremendous roar went up on the ship and Hannah realized the prisoners were cheering for them.

The British soldiers scrambled down the rope ladder into the ship's boat. "They're launching a boat," Hannah shouted.

"They will overtake us for sure," Dobbs said. "We need to get to land. We'll have a better chance to hide."

"The bank by the shore is too high and muddy for us to climb," Daniel said.

Still weak from smallpox and the shock of the freezing water, Hannah's body trembled violently as she doggedly pulled on the oars. Dobbs gave her a worried look, but he could not afford to lose time taking her place at the oars. Then the river curved and for a few moments they were out of sight.

"Look ahead," Daniel finally gasped. He pointed to a small marshy inlet with a stand of cattails nearly blocking it. Dobbs nodded, "Just what we need." Using the oars, they maneuvered the boat until it was hidden among the reeds. "This might give us a little time."

A light snow was in the air, but fortunately not enough of it was sticking to the ground to show their tracks. Hannah's teeth chattered and her legs felt numb. Although the clothes were dry, they were thin and worn and offered little protection from the frigid wind. Hannah saw that Daniel's lips were still blue. "Head for those woods," Dobbs said, leading the way. Bending against the wind, they ran through a flat, swampy area with reed-filled ponds. A startled pair of wild geese took to the air with a flapping of wings and noisy honks that nearly made Hannah's heart stop until she realized what it was. They reached a thick forest cut through with deep ravines. Suddenly Daniel sank to the ground shaking helplessly. "I can't go on," he mumbled.

Far away, Hannah could hear the faint shouts of the British as they climbed on shore.

"Yes, you can," she said fiercely. "Do you want to die?" she half pushed, half pulled Daniel through the woods. At last they slid down into a deep ravine.

"It will be dark in a few minutes," Dobbs whispered. "I don't think the British will go tramping about in the woods at night."

"I smell smoke," Hannah said quietly.

"I do too," Daniel said. "Sorry, I started to give up back there."

"It's okay. I can barely move myself," Hannah said.

"I think I'm alright now. Stay here. I'm going to go check on that smoke."

"Be careful," Hannah whispered.

Nodding, Daniel worked his way up the ravine, melting into the growing darkness. Just after Daniel had left, Dobbs put his finger across Hannah's mouth. At the same time, he pushed her down and flattened himself against the steep side of the ravine. Above them, Hannah could hear the sound of men passing. Two of them paused almost directly above where Dobbs and Hannah were hidden in the deep shadows. Hannah clenched her teeth, sure they would be able to hear the uncontrollable shaking of her body. She thought of Daniel and swallowed the fear that rose in her throat.

"It's too dark to continue the search," one of the soldiers above them remarked. "With no shelter, they won't last long. We'll find their lifeless bodies in the spring, I'll wager."

The other one grunted. "We don't know they even headed this way. The people around here are loyal. They will turn them in if they see them. If they're not loyal, the prison ships are a good reminder. There's a tavern nearby. I suggest we warm up with a glass of ale." The men were standing on the edge of the ravine and pebbles rained down heavily on Dobbs and Hannah until the men finally walked away.

After a few minutes, Hannah dared to whisper. "What if Daniel runs into them?"

"Then Daniel will hide," said Daniel's whispered voice. "They were so noisy I had plenty of warning."

"What did you find?" Dobbs said.

"There's a road not far from the end of this ravine. I saw a few houses."

With Daniel in the lead they made their way through

the ravine. Ahead of them was a cobblestone road. Smoke curled from the chimneys of several houses along the way.

Dobbs crouched low and muttered, "We have to decide what to do. The other side of the river is Manhattan Island, where, according to the men on the prison ship, there are thousands of British soldiers. There might be fewer soldiers here, but chances are most of the people around here are loyalists. They would turn us in instantly. There might even be soldiers billeted in some of the houses."

"The British are forcing these people to provide food and lodging to their soldiers? How horrible!" Hannah said. Then she pointed to a house that sat farther back from the road than the others. "Wait! That house has a big barn. Maybe we could at least get out of the wind while we make plans."

Nodding in agreement, they raced across the road, circling around to the barn. Through the windows, Hannah could see a woman sitting at a table polishing silver. It all seemed so normal and common, and yet just a short distance away were the terrible prison ships.

They had managed to stay hidden in the woods, but now they had to cross open land to reach the barn. Looking around, Hannah saw no one. The woman in the house was still intent on her chore, and although thick smoke came from the chimneys of the nearby houses, there was no other sign of life. At a nudge from Dobbs, she ran again.

They reached the barn door, pulled open the latch, and stepped inside.

It was dreadfully cold, but at least they were out of the wind. There was a tall stack of hay in the corner and a brown and white cow in a pen. Daniel stumbled into a few chickens, sending them running about in a frenzy of squawks. Hannah, Daniel, and Dobbs stayed still until the fowl settled back down. They then climbed into the hay and clung to each other for warmth.

"I can't believe we made it," Hannah said softly.

"If we don't find a better way to get warm, we are not going to make it," Dobbs warned. "I don't know how much more of this our bodies can stand."

The door suddenly creaked open. A woman stood there holding a lantern in one hand and a pistol in the other. It was the same woman Hannah had seen in the farmhouse window. Although Hannah could see laugh lines at the corners of the woman's mouth, she did not look friendly now. She waved the pistol at them. "Get out of there you varmints. Thought you could take advantage of a poor widow woman, did you?"

chapter eleven

Trapped

Dobbs stood up slowly. "Careful with that gun, woman," he said. "We meant you no harm. We only wanted to get warm."

The woman was silent as she inspected them in the faint winter light. "You've escaped from that prison ship," she said, her eyes narrowing. "Are they after you?"

"Yes," Dobbs said.

"There will be a reward, no doubt," the woman said thoughtfully.

Hannah stood up and faced the woman. "Please don't send us back. You have no idea how terrible it was—rotten food, no heat, sickness and death every day. Then we swam through that terrible cold water. Don't let it be for nothing."

The woman tapped the side of her chin with the pistol, deep in thought. "I could be hanged for helping you," she said slowly.

"If you can't help us, at least don't turn us in," Daniel pleaded.

Suddenly they could hear shouts and the sounds of horses' hooves. Seeming to reach a decision, the woman quickly opened a barely visible trapdoor. "Get down there now."

Hannah's heart pounded. Did the woman mean to capture them? Trapped in a fruit cellar they would have no way to escape if she told the soldiers.

"Quickly," the woman whispered frantically.

The voices were getting closer, so Hannah and her friends had no choice but to trust the woman. They scrambled down a rickety wooden ladder to a small room with a dirt floor. Before the woman closed the door Hannah saw shelves full of preserves, apples, potatoes, carrots, and turnips. Then they were plunged into darkness and Hannah could hear the sound of hay bales being dragged over the trapdoor.

"Don't move," Dobbs whispered urgently. "If we bump into those shelves they will hear for sure." Hannah froze. She heard the clank above her, and then a dull thump. Just as soldiers burst into the barn, Hannah heard the sound of hooves stamping on the old wooden floor above them.

The voices were muffled, but Hannah could make out the conversation. "We are looking for escaped prisoners," a man shouted.

"Oh my," the woman answered, sounding shocked and worried. "Are they dangerous? I am a poor widow."

"You have seen nothing?" the soldier asked.

"Nothing," she said. "Although I did hear dogs barking near the village a short time ago."

"Check the haystack," one of the soldiers said. *Thwack, thwack* sounded the pitchfork prongs as they were stabbed into the hay bales. Hannah held her breath. If they hit the wooden door of the fruit cellar they would feel the difference from the dirt floor of the barn. After a minute the sounds stopped. Apparently satisfied no one was in the barn, the soldier said, "You're late with your milking."

Hannah heard the stream of milk hitting the side of the bucket.

"Bessy did not give much earlier," the woman answered calmly.

"Very well. Be sure to report any suspicious activity." Hannah heard the sound of boots. At the door they suddenly stopped. "Keep your door locked, widow. These are desperate men."

"I am sure you will capture them," the woman said. "As for myself, three of your officers are billeted at my house. I am sure they will protect me."

After a few minutes, the woman called softly. "Best to stay there. The British officers usually go to the tavern in the village after dinner. I will come when it is safe."

Hannah sat on the floor trembling with cold. Daniel felt around until he found three apples. He put his arm around Hannah and handed her and Dobbs each an apple. Dobbs sat on the other side, but even sitting close together, Hannah could not stop shaking.

The hours dragged slowly by. Hannah dozed in fits and starts, but finally, the widow returned and lifted the door. "They usually stay at the tavern for a short time. I've brought you some warmer clothes and a little food. That's all I can do. I don't fancy getting my neck stretched."

As they climbed out of their hiding spot, the woman said, "I listened to their conversation at dinner. They think you may be headed for Manhattan Island, planning to get across the Hudson to New Jersey. They are watching for you there."

"That's good to know," Dobbs said.

She had brought them warm underwear and woolen shirts. The woman peeked nervously out the door while they changed. Dobbs and Daniel turned their backs and Hannah quickly put on the clean clothes. "Those were my husband's clothes," she called, still looking out the door. "The British killed him."

The husband had been about the same size as Dobbs. The clothes were baggy on Hannah and Daniel, but at least they were all warm and their bodies no longer shook with the cold. The woman gathered up the old clothes. "I will burn them. Now go and good luck to you," she said, handing Dobbs the pistol. "It doesn't work, but no one will know. It fooled you. I don't know what else I can do to help you."

"You have already done more than we could have imagined," Dobbs said.

"This road will lead you to Albany. It is still in rebel hands, I hear. But beware, there are many soldiers about."

Drawing her blanket around her, Hannah stepped out into the night. It was sharply cold and the clear sky was sprinkled with enough stars to light their way. The woman latched the barn door and hurried back to the house.

As they reached the trees they heard laughter and the steady clip-clop of horses' hooves on the cobblestone road. Crouching low, they ducked back into the ravine where they had hidden before, just as three British soldiers rode into view.

"Did you see something?" one of them said loudly.

Hannah held her breath, until at last another voice, this one slurred with drink, said, "A deer, no doubt. Who else would be out in this cold? Let's go in and warm ourselves by Widow McCracken's fire."

Hannah, Daniel, and Dobbs listened as the officers tended their horses and at last staggered into the house. Hannah allowed herself to breathe normally.

"We could wait until they are asleep and then steal the horses," Daniel suggested.

Dobbs nodded, but Hannah spoke. "I think we should go see if the boat is still there. We can make good time on the river and if we stay close to the high banks we are not likely to be seen."

"I think that's a good plan," Dobbs said, unable to hide the relief in his voice. "I've never ridden a horse before. We're sailors. We should stay with what we know."

Silently they hurried back to the marshy cove where they had left the boat that afternoon. So much had happened that Hannah found it difficult to believe that it had only been a few hours since they swam in the icy water and escaped. Now, they were fed and clothed in good woolen clothes. If their luck held and the boat was undiscovered, they might actually escape.

Dobbs had taken the lead, but suddenly he held up his hand to stop Daniel and Hannah. "Let me go ahead and scout around," he whispered. "You two stay here." Before they could protest, he was gone.

They sat down, hidden by tall grass. Hannah listened intently, but the only sound was the gentle slap of water against the banks and a far-off hoot of an owl. Then she heard the rustle of grass and Dobbs was back. "The boat is still there," he whispered so softly she could scarcely hear. "There are four soldiers camped nearby. They've dug a trench and I would have stumbled right into it if one of them had not coughed. Also, there is a British ship heading up the river. They must patrol the river at night."

"I say we try to take the soldiers," Hannah said. "I am tired of running and hiding."

"How could we take four armed soldiers, with one broken pistol?" Daniel asked.

"I think Hannah is right," Dobbs said slowly. "If there are soldiers here, there are probably some on the road too. Sooner or later we are going to run into them. They won't be expecting us to attack, so we have surprise on our side."

"We had better not do anything until the ship is well past," Daniel said. "The soldiers might be giving it a signal."

Daniel was right. As the ship slid silently past, plainly visible in the glow of lanterns on deck, a soldier climbed out of the trench. Standing on the bank he slowly waved a white cloth. Then, instead of heading back to the trench, he walked in the opposite direction.

Hannah grabbed the pistol. "He's going to relieve himself," she whispered. Before Daniel or Dobbs could stop her she raced through the grass, remaining as silent as the wind. The soldier had laid his weapon in the ground and was refastening his trousers.

Coming up behind the soldier, she shoved the gun in his back. "Stay silent if you want to live," she said. He froze and Hannah picked up his weapon. Prodding him with the bayonet, she led him back to Dobbs and Daniel.

While they decided what to do next, a British voice shouted hoarsely. "John, where are you?"

"Groan. Tell him you fell and twisted your foot and you need help." Hannah prodded her prisoner. "No tricks."

The soldier followed Hannah's directions, evidently deciding that living was better than warning his friends. Daniel and Dobbs took the soldier's weapon from Hannah. Pretending the broken pistol was good, Daniel gave it to Hannah and said, "If he moves, shoot him." Hannah nodded as Dobbs and Daniel disappeared into the tall marsh grass along the shore. Hannah took a fierce stance. Fortunately, only a minute later, Dobbs and Daniel were back with the second soldier and another captured weapon.

"Let's try that again. Tell them he is too heavy," she instructed the second captive. "Tell them you need more help. Don't try to warn them or you'll die."

This time she had an actual weapon, but she still stood grimly waiting to see if their ruse would work again. The bold trick was successful. Leading the third soldier, Daniel came back, and a second later Dobbs returned with the last soldier. “They had some rope,” he said. “Tie them up.”

“It will be morning before we are found,” the British soldier named John complained.

“After the way we have been treated, you’re lucky that we are leaving you alive,” Daniel said, as he gathered up the weapons.

The soldiers remained quiet after that and Hannah and Dobbs soon had them tied too tightly to escape anytime soon. Hannah, Daniel, and Dobbs had left the boat wedged tightly among the reeds. They stowed their packs and their newly captured weapons, each with a bayonet attached and took one last quick look around. “Good luck to us,” Dobbs said as he picked up one set of oars and Daniel the other.

“I can row,” Hannah protested.

“You can relieve us later,” Daniel offered. “For now you be the lookout. Keep a sharp eye on the banks and watch for that ship. It may come back.”

“Do you know where we’re going?” Hannah whispered.

“Albany,” Dobbs said. “Like the widow said, Albany’s still in American hands. I believe this river goes that way. From there, we can make our way to Portsmouth.”

Dobbs and Daniel rowed steadily, trying to keep their efforts as silent as possible. Even so, Hannah worried that they could be heard by anyone along the bank. Luck was with them, however. Except for a small herd of deer browsing in the tall shore grass they saw no other signs of life. After several hours, Hannah's eyes ached from her vigilance. The river narrowed and she saw there was a long island in the middle. It was heavily forested and seemed deserted. After a time, she relieved Daniel first, and then Dobbs. Although her hands, grown soft from the months in prison, soon began to blister, she was happy to be doing her share of the work.

Dobbs took back the oars and whispered, "It will be dawn soon. We need to find a place to rest."

"Sooner than you think," Hannah whispered back. "Look."

A faint light twinkled on the water moving closer as they watched. "It's that blasted English ship coming back," Daniel hissed.

Every second brought the light closer. Hannah looked around, fighting to stay calm. "I think I see a little cove on the island there."

"I see it too," Dobbs said. They maneuvered the boat toward the island shore as they pulled frantically on the oars. Hannah could now see the faint outline of a ship heading straight for them.

The tall trees on the island loomed. Hannah's teeth were clenched, but she was hardly aware of it. Every second she expected a shout from the ship or the sound of a cannon being readied to fire. Suddenly, the ship disappeared from view and she realized that her little boat had slipped into the cove. Dobbs grunted with effort as they rowed the last few strokes to the island.

"Quick! Get the boat on shore," he said, leaping out and tugging the boat onto the forested shore. Daniel and Hannah jumped out also and each taking a side they carried the boat deep into the forest.

The sky had begun to lighten, and as the English ship sailed back down the river Dobbs, Daniel, and Hannah watched anxiously from their hiding place in the thick forest. The ship was lit with lanterns. It was a small ship but heavily armed. In addition to the cannon there were two smaller guns mounted on swivels, and three men stood ready at each one. Two sailors picked up ship's glasses and, standing on either side of the ship, began to scan the shores. Another sailor was already at watch from the crow's nest, the perch high up on the main mast. Even though Hannah knew it was too dark to be seen from their hiding place in the forest, she instinctively ducked back behind the trees. She noticed that Dobbs and Daniel had done the same thing. Hannah's stomach churned and she tasted angry bile at the sight of the English ship sailing unchallenged on American waters. It had been over three years since the Colonies had declared their independence. She made a silent vow that she would somehow get back in the fight until the country was free from British domination and every English soldier was driven from the country.

The first pink streaks of sunrise showed on the horizon as the ship slowly sailed out of view. Hannah, Daniel, and Dobbs stood up and stretched wearily, stamping their frozen feet to warm them. Dobbs unwrapped one of the packages Widow McCracken had made for them and passed out hunks of bread and cheese.

Hannah ate hers slowly, savoring the taste of the bread while she looked around. "What shall we do now?" she asked, drawing a blanket around her against the bitter cold.

"I don't know about you young'uns," Dobbs said. "But I need some rest. I suggest we walk around a bit, make sure there are no surprises, and then find a place to sleep."

"Surprises?" Hannah asked.

"People," Daniel answered for Dobbs. "The island looks deserted, but let's make sure. Maybe we can find someplace sheltered to make a camp."

"We'll split up," Dobbs said. "Look for any sign people are around. A trail, woodchips from cutting, anything like that. Be careful."

Dobbs and Daniel set off in different directions. A small stream bubbled down into the cove. Hannah hopped over it and set off though the woods, stopping now and then to listen. If there were any houses on the island she should be able to smell wood smoke, but the air was fresh and heavy with the scent of pine. This part of the island was higher, and Hannah climbed around several outcroppings of granite. A small bluff caught her interest and after climbing over the rocks she discovered a shallow cave. With a bed of pine boughs, it would make a perfect shelter. She hurried back to the boat to meet the others.

Dobbs and Daniel arrived a few minutes later and she led them back to her discovery. “Well done!” Dobbs said, as he set about stripping some low branches and spreading them thickly on the cave floor. “We’ll take turns standing guard.”

“I’ll go first,” Hannah said. “I’m wide awake.” Daniel gave her a grateful look and curled up on the fragrant bed of pine, wrapping his blanket tightly around him. Even before Dobbs settled down, Hannah heard the soft sound of a snore coming from Daniel. “Don’t let us sleep too long,” Dobbs said. “You will need rest too. Watch the sun and wake me at noon.”

Hannah nodded. Remembering the wretched prison ships, she leaned back against the rocks determined to guard her sleeping friends better than on the island where they had buried the treasure. They had thought they were alone then too. She stood up and stretched to keep herself awake, then climbed to the top of the bluff where she had a clear view of the river.

With the extra height and the clear light of day, she could see, to her amazement, that the river curved into a huge bay. So that was where the English ship had been able to turn to sail back down the other direction. Several large islands dotted the bay, and here and there a haze of smoke suggested small towns or at least a settlement of some kind.

Hannah strained, trying to see, wishing she had the ship's glass to help. Around one side of the bay there appeared to be a small town, and at the water's edge a small sailing ship was anchored. It was so far away it looked like a child's toy boat. On the land there were several buildings and what appeared to be another ship, this one on its side as though it was being repaired. She watched for a while until she was sure. It was a boatyard. But was it British or American? If it was American, was it run by Tories? There was no way to be sure. One thing was certain: if it was a boatyard then there was an opening to the sea. She looked up at the sun—too soon to wake up and tell Daniel and Dobbs.

A rattle of pebbles alerted her to footsteps behind her. She grabbed her gun and swung around only to see Daniel rubbing sleep out of his eyes.

Daniel chuckled as he sat down on the rocks. "I'm glad I'm not a British soldier. You look pretty serious with that weapon."

"I've been sitting here thinking all morning. I know the smart thing to do is head for Albany," said Hannah. "But the sight of that patrol ship and those smug British sailors with their fancy uniforms makes me wish we could just blow them out of the water."

Daniel held up three fingers. "There are only three of us, remember?"

"I know," Hannah said with a glum look. "I still wish we could think of something."

"I couldn't sleep any longer," Daniel said. "I'll take the watch. You go sleep."

Hannah took the spot Daniel had vacated, nestling in the fragrant boughs. Beside her, Dobbs snored heartily, seemingly unaffected by the cold. The thin blanket offered little protection from the cold, but Hannah pulled it tightly around her and closed her eyes.

It was nearly dark when Daniel shook her. "Wake up, you lazy sailor," he teased.

Dobbs handed out the rest of the bread and cheese. "We talked while you were sleeping. We have a plan, but we are all in this together, so we all need to agree."

Hannah nodded as Dobbs continued. "The British are very orderly and exact. I think the ship will come by at about the same time tonight. That gives us time to get to the other side of the river close to the shipyard. If it looks safe we'll go into town and try to buy some food."

Dobbs saw that Hannah was about to protest and held up his hand. "I know you and Daniel think we should try to take the ship, but we don't know why it's there. I don't want to get aboard and discover it has a broken rudder. We came a long way on the river. Albany can't be that far. Or maybe we can find the Boston Post Road and head that way. If we can find a road we might even be able to get a ride to Albany."

Hannah sighed. She knew Dobbs was right. Still she felt disappointed. She could see that Daniel was dissatisfied with the decision also, although he did not express it. They carried the boat from its hiding place in the woods and launched it from the cove. They had rowed close to the shipyard when once again they saw the English ship. The bank was too high to scramble ashore without being seen so they sat without moving, hiding in some tall reeds. The English ship passed, its show of might wasted on the town with houses shuttered and dark.

Hannah, Daniel, and Dobbs were forced to stay in their dark sheltered spot as the ship made its slow turn and headed back down the river. "I don't suppose we should arrive in town in the middle of the night," Daniel said.

"I've been thinking," Dobbs offered, "tomorrow I will say that I am a doctor traveling to Albany to set up a practice. You are my children."

Hannah giggled. "Yes, Papa."

"This is serious," Dobbs said sternly. "I don't know if we are still behind enemy lines, but if we are and get caught, we could be hanged as spies."

"I know," Hannah said quietly.

Dobbs sighed. "I shouldn't have snapped at you. We're all in this together. I'm just not used to all this skulking about on land. The sea is where I belong," he added. "Plus, I've grown fond of the two of you."

"We'll be careful," Daniel promised.

At dawn they rowed closer to the town. They found a beach not far from the shipyard, and landed the boat, "I don't think we will use the boat again, but let's drag it to those reeds and hide it," Dobbs said. "We'll leave the weapons too so we don't attract attention in town."

That task done, they hid and watched the small town come alive. There were several streets of sturdy brick houses, a church, a general store, and a building Hannah thought might be a school. With the light of day, men came out of some of the houses, heading for the shipyard. Children, carrying baskets of lunch, waved to their mothers and went to the schoolhouse. Hannah watched them enviously. Although her mother had taught her how to read and write, she had never been able to go to a real school.

A portly man wearing a white apron came out of a house and unlocked the doors to the general store right next door. There was no sign of British soldiers about.

"Let's go," Dobbs said, leading the way.

"I am going to look around town a bit," Daniel said suddenly. "Maybe I'll see if there is any work at the shipyard."

Dobbs hesitated and then warned, "Be careful."

A few minutes later Dobbs and Hannah pushed open the door of the general store and walked in. The proprietor had already started a good fire in the iron stove in the middle of the room. Hannah stood by it, gratefully warming her hands. The storekeeper looked up and tried to smile despite a dreadfully swollen jaw. "You are strangers in town," he said. "I haven't seen you before."

Dobbs told him the story they had practiced and the man nodded. "You can follow the post trail. It's not a good road but it leads back along the Hudson River. Just follow that and you will come to the road. One way goes to Albany, the other to Boston."

"Are there a lot of British around?" Dobbs asked.

The man looked at them, taking their measure before he replied. "There are some here to guard the shipyard. The way you are going there are not many past West Point. Our boys strung a giant chain clear across the river. Another traveler told me each link in the chain weighs

125 pounds. Floated it across with rafts. The British can't figure out how to get around it."

Hannah exchanged a look with Dobbs. They had no way to warn Daniel that British soldiers were about. The shake of Dobbs's head was almost imperceptible, as he warned her to stay calm.

"That's a pretty bad tooth you have there," Dobbs said. "I can pull it for you."

"I'll take you up on that," the storekeeper said. "I'll give you some supplies in return. Let me fetch my wife to run to the store for a bottle of rum."

The man went next door, returning in a few minutes with his wife, who was equally plump and friendly. She poured her husband a large drink to dull the pain.

"Do all the men in town work at the shipyard?" Dobbs asked, while they waited for the drink to take effect.

The storekeeper took another drink. "Most of them," he said. "They used to make fishing boats, fine-crafted boats known all through these waters. The British put a stop to that. They wanted us to repair their ships. Said if we didn't they would send more soldiers."

"What about that ship at anchor?" Hannah asked.

"British merchant ship for the trade in the Bermudas," the storekeeper explained. "They completely refurbished its inside. I heard the captain will be here with a crew tomorrow to fetch it."

"Is there a back room, goodwife?" Dobbs asked. "And I will need pliers."

The storekeeper's wife helped her husband to a chair in a back room full of boxes and barrels. From a supply of tools in the store she selected a sturdy pair of pliers.

"Hold him still," Dobbs instructed.

Hannah held one side of him and his wife the other. When the storekeeper opened his mouth, the odor of infection and rum was so strong it made Hannah feel faint. She wondered how Dobbs could stand it. Dobbs did not even flinch. He peered in the storekeeper's mouth and, after deciding which tooth to pull, reached in with the pliers. With a roar, the storekeeper tried to come out of his chair so that it took every bit of Hannah's strength to hold him still. Dobbs wiggled and pulled, finally bracing one knee on the man's lap. At last, with one mighty tug, the tooth came free. Dobbs held up the black tooth.

"You are lucky," he said. "It came out all in one piece."

The storekeeper mumbled something that sounded like he didn't feel lucky, but Dobbs handed him another drink of rum, instructing him to gargle with it and then spit it out.

"He'll be hurting for a time until that swelling goes down," Dobbs told the man's wife. "Rinsing with salt water aids in the healing."

"My husband instructed me to give you the supplies you need," she said, giving them a shrewd look. "I heard all your questions about the ship and I can tell by your walk that you are sailors. Are you planning on taking the ship? You need not worry about me. The whole town is afraid that when the English captain arrives it will be with soldiers to force our young men into service. Everyone would be grateful if that ship disappeared."

Not waiting for an answer, she went on. "The British left payment for supplies. They are stacked on the dock. There is food for the galley and wood for the stove."

"Won't the British hold the town responsible?" Dobbs asked.

"How could they? We know nothing. We were asleep in our beds."

Hannah and Dobbs helped the woman take her husband to his bed and left to find Daniel. They had no more than stepped outside when they saw Daniel hurrying toward them with another man.

"This is Thomas Bishop," he said when he caught up to them. "He wants to help us take the ship. And he says there are others who will join us."

"You don't want to make a move until after the patrol ship comes around," Thomas said earnestly. "They signal them with lanterns."

"How many British are here?" Dobbs asked.

"There are eight," Thomas told them. When their faces fell he hastened to add, "There is a small barracks. Four of them sleep while the others patrol."

"How many men do you think you can get to help?" Hannah asked. Thomas counted silently on his fingers. "At least nine. All sailors. This used to be a fishing village. We have few weapons though. The British took them."

Dobbs nodded. "We'll go back to the boat. You round up the men and meet us there." As Thomas started to leave Dobbs warned, "Approach the woods from different directions a few at a time. We don't need anyone noticing."

Thomas grinned and nodded as he hurried away.

chapter twelve

Attack!

It was a long day, but true to Thomas Bishop's word, the men arrived. They slipped quietly through the woods in ones and twos, each with a bundle of belongings. The men sat on the ground, waiting and making plans, until finally it was dark and the patrol boat had made its rounds.

At last Dobbs stood up. "We need to take each man singly. We don't have enough weapons to sustain a fight. Once you've captured the guards, bring us a couple of the guns and we will rush the men in the barracks." He passed out the four weapons they had confiscated from the British soldiers, letting Hannah keep the broken pistol.

"We'll signal like this," Thomas said, perfectly imitating an owl.

"Good. As soon as we hear that, we will take the men in the barracks," Dobbs said, motioning for Hannah and Daniel to follow him.

Hannah shivered with excitement. She could hardly believe what was happening. If all went well, they would soon be sailing to Portsmouth to find Mr. Gaines.

Silently they approached the shipyard, crouching in the tall shore grass. They could see several of the soldiers, marching smartly back and forth, the faint moonlight glinting on the bayonets attached to their guns. Hannah felt a moment of despair. The soldiers were well trained and heavily armed. As though he had read her thoughts, Thomas whispered cheerfully, "Don't worry. Those soldiers never played hide and seek along this shore."

In a flash the men separated, two by two, circling the yard. Dobbs pointed to a good-sized building. A faint glow of a lantern came from a small window. "That must be the barracks," he whispered.

Suddenly from the far corner of the yard came a faint "whoo whoo" sound of an owl. To one side they heard a scuffle, then another owl hoot. There were a few anxious moments before the third and fourth signals came.

They waited for the men to bring their prisoners, but suddenly the door of the barracks opened and a soldier stepped out stretching and yawning. He started to go back inside and then stopped as though puzzled. He took a few steps away from the building, peering into the night. If he saw the men returning with the prisoners he could shout an alarm. Without thinking, Hannah grabbed the only weapon nearby, the broken pistol, and ran silently up behind the soldier. At the last second he heard her and turned, but Hannah stood up and leveled her weapon. "Don't move," she said.

Daniel and Dobbs arrived with guns. "Good work," Dobbs said softly. He and Daniel burst through the door. For just a moment there was shouting, and then the last three soldiers came out, wearing only their long underwear.

"Find some rope. Lots of it," Dobbs said tersely.

Several of Thomas's men scattered and soon returned with rope. They took the British prisoners into the barracks and tied them securely.

The barracks had one room with bunks and a small kitchen. Hannah opened another door and her eyes widened in surprise. Several barrels of gunpowder were stored there. "Dobbs, come and look," she shouted.

Dobbs looked pleased. "We'll take it with us. At least if we are attacked we can put up a fight."

Leaving one man to guard the British soldiers, the men started ferrying the supplies to the ship. With only one small boat it took a long time back and forth, and Dobbs kept an anxious eye on the night sky watching for the first signs of dawn.

From the dock, Hannah helped Thomas Bishop and Dobbs load supplies for the galley and row them to the ship.

It was too dark to see the name painted on the hull. "She's called the *Elizabeth*," Thomas said. "After an English queen."

"We'll rename her soon as we get into safer waters," Dobbs promised.

Once on board, Hannah lit a lantern and set to work stocking the galley. When the job was nearly done she took the lantern and explored the ship. On the gun deck she found eight big guns, each with a row of cannonballs and supplies beside them. She then went to find Dobbs.

It was starting to snow, which would help shield them, but also made the deck slippery. Dobbs was supervising the last load, the barrels of gunpowder and linen bags for the cartridges.

"We are about ready to go," he said, looking at the first streaks of dawn in the horizon. "And just in time."

"I have an idea," Hannah said.

Hearing the serious tone in her voice, Dobbs put down the box he was carrying and looked at her. "Why do I have this feeling I don't want to hear your idea?" he asked.

Daniel walked by rolling a barrel of water for the galley. "What is going on?" he said, seeing their tense expressions.

"Jack is about to tell me how we should attack the patrol ship," Dobbs said.

Hannah grinned. "So you are thinking about it too."

"Thought about it and dismissed it," Dobbs said.

"I think it is a great idea," Daniel said. "It would make up for all those months rotting on that prison ship."

"Not if we're all dead," Dobbs said, picking up his box.

"I've thought it all out," Hannah said. "We can have the guns armed and ready. They won't be expecting anything, so we will take them completely by surprise."

"Jack's right," said Daniel. "In battle, captains always try to cross the bow of the other ship. They will be heading right for us, so they will be in that position."

"One gun aimed at the forward swivel guns. One to take out the main mast. One shot into their gun deck," Hannah counted on her fingers. "And one," she said, holding up the last finger, "One low enough to make them take on water."

"You forget we don't have a trained gun crew," Dobbs said, looking thoughtful.

"We've got some time," Hannah said.

Dobbs put down the box again and threw up his hands in surrender. "Take a vote. We won't do it unless the new crew agrees. And find out if any of them have experience with big guns," he called out as they hurried away to round up the crew.

Hannah's idea was met with a rousing cheer. Luckily, two of the men had experience. One had worked on a merchant ship and Thomas Bishop had actually served on an English ship. "I can help load the guns," Thomas told them. "But you will have one chance. The English have the best navy in the world. It is because they practice every day. They can fire a gun every three minutes. We will have one chance to do whatever damage we can. The forward swivel guns will be loaded and ready. We have to take them out, do whatever damage we can in the next few minutes, and get out of here fast."

The new crew listened gravely. Working together, the guns were soon loaded with powder, cartridge, ball, and canvas wadding, and aimed where they thought the ship would make its turn.

"Even if we are lucky enough to cripple them, they may try to fight back," Dobbs said. "As soon as we've fired our rounds, unfurl the sails and raise the anchor."

"They're coming," Thomas called softly.

The patrol boat was barely visible through the swirling snow. Hannah hid with the rest of the small crew waiting for the ship moving slowly towards them. Her mind was in turmoil. The English ship could easily have a crew of fifty men. It had been her idea to fight. There had already been so much senseless loss of life the past few months—Jonesy, Ratso, Samuel Stewart, Shorty, and likely Captain Nelson. Hannah didn't want to be responsible for the death or imprisonment of Daniel, Dobbs, and her new friends.

"Steady," Dobbs called softly.

"Wait," Hannah cried. "They are coming in too far over. Our guns are aimed too high. If we fire them we will miss the forward guns."

The men with experience on gun crews checked the sights. "Jack is right," one of them said.

There was a moment of silence. If the men moved to aim the guns again they would surely be seen. "We don't have a choice," Dobbs said. "Pray the snow covers us."

Four men grabbed the heavy cannons and ever so slightly adjusted the aim. Hannah was on the first gun, the one aimed at the crucial forward guns. She pushed with every bit of her strength until slowly the heavy guns were slid into the right position.

From the gun ports they could see sudden activity on the deck of the patrol ship.

"They have either seen us or have noticed something on shore," Daniel said.

But they were as ready as they could be. Dobbs held up his hand. The powder was pierced and the flintlock fired, and with a mighty roar the first gun jumped into action. The men held their breath as the ball flew through space, hitting the British guns dead center. Then suddenly a terrific explosion was seen.

"We did it!" Hannah screamed. A cheer went up from the men. Then before the ringing in her ears had stopped, the second gun was fired and, immediately after, the third and fourth.

The English ship was badly damaged, but it was obvious there were still men left to fight. A hail of shots flew toward the *Elizabeth,* and British sailors could be seen launching their ship's boat.

"We need to sail before they can get any of those big guns loaded," Thomas yelled. With several men to help, he raced to raise the anchor. Hannah hurried to the deck and nimbly started to climb the lines of the main mast, ignoring the musket balls whizzing past her. Daniel was beside her climbing the mizzenmast. Suddenly she felt a searing pain on the side of her head. A thin trickle of blood ran down her face and she clung to the lines, fighting a wave of nausea.

"You're hit," Daniel cried out.

Hannah wiped her eyes, "It's nothing," she said, continuing to climb.

"Cover us," Daniel shouted. Dobbs had already seen what was happening. With their captured weapons Dobbs and two others knelt along the rail, firing back as Hannah and Daniel reached the top and unfurled the sails.

"Look," Daniel shouted. "We did it."

The English ship was listing badly. The sailors were abandoning the ship, fighting to lower the ship's boats.

Hannah's small crew jumped and cheered with jubilation, pounding each other on the back and grinning with pride and relief. As the *Elizabeth* slowly moved out to sea, Hannah watched from her perch with satisfaction. *We will keep this up until every last one of them goes back to England,* she thought as she climbed back down to the main deck.

"Let me look at that wound," Dobbs said. He wrapped a bandage around her head. "It's nothing serious; the ball just grazed you. Although another inch over and you would be dead. Except for one man who had a toe crushed from the gun recoil, we are all well. With people like you, the British haven't a chance."

"Like us," Hannah said.

Dobbs nodded. "Like us," he agreed.

"Hey, Jack. Dobbs and I agreed on a name for the ship." Before Hannah could protest that they hadn't asked her opinion, he said, "First chance we get, we are going to name her the *Hannah*. We told the crew it was after a really brave girl the three of us know."

Hannah lowered her head to hide the sudden blush of pleasure at the honor. "Dobbs, Daniel, and I talked about something while we were waiting for you all to arrive yesterday," she announced to the new crew. "Until we get to Portsmouth, Dobbs will act as captain. When we reach Portsmouth we believe the first mate from our old ship the

Sea Hawk will be waiting there with the first ship we captured. Anyone who wants to stay in Portsmouth can, and good luck to you. For those of you who choose to stay with us, we will take the two ships—and more, if we can find them—and head for the Carolinas. There's a treasure hidden there, and those who help will be rewarded with half a share. All the time we are sailing we will practice so that our gun crews are as good as any on a British ship. When we have our treasure we will take our revenge for the *Sea Hawk* and all the men who still suffer on those accursed prison ships. We intend to keep fighting until every English ship is driven from our waters."

The men cheered. "We're with you, Jack!"

"Then let's get to work, sailors," said Dobbs. "We've got a treasure to find and a war to win."

"Aye, aye!" they all said.

The Real History Behind the Story

Hannah is a fictional character, but most of the things that happen to her are based on fact.

Food at Sea

Food onboard sailing ships was often not much better than the prisoner's food, although portions were more generous. Sailors ate mostly salted beef, soaked to remove the salt and then boiled; pease, which was a general term for dried peas or beans; and ship's biscuits, or hardtack, so hard they had to be soaked to eat. Breakfast was generally oatmeal, which after a few weeks was usually infested with weevils. Flummery was a bland pudding, considered to be a treat. Water, stored in wooden barrels, often became slimy. Sailors were happy when the ships stopped at islands for fresh water, greens, turtles, and fruit.

Wartime Prisons

At the beginning of the Revolutionary War, when General William Howe captured New York, thousands of men, women, and children who had helped the rebels were arrested. Sometimes their only crime was refusing to swear allegiance to the British Crown.

There was a standing offer that any man who would serve in the British Navy would be freed. Very few did. Most remained loyal to the United States, choosing to suffer under unimaginable conditions and die rather than betray their cause. These men were true heroes and patriots and yet few people know of their sacrifice and they are seldom mentioned in history books.

William Cunningham was in charge of hanging Nathan Hale, an American spy in 1776. Cunningham treated his prisoners brutally and had many Americans hanged.

The British were faced with the problem of where to put an estimated five thousand prisoners. Several buildings, jails, churches, and sugar houses (factories to refine the sugar cane brought from the Caribbean islands), were used, but there were so many prisoners that the crowded conditions were deplorable.

General Howe made William Cunningham provost marshal, the person in charge of the military police. Part of his job was to provide for the prisoners. Cunningham was a small-time thug who had once been humiliated by the patriots. He bought the cheapest food he could—spoiled meat, bug-infested grain, and rancid oil—and kept the money he saved. Cunningham was the man in charge of hanging Nathan Hale, an American spy famous for saying, "I only regret I have but one life to give for my country." In addition to the legal hangings, Cunningham is reported to have killed another 250 men in secret nighttime hangings.

The Prison Ships

Because the patriots had a very small navy, other ships were offered letters of marque, giving them permission to prey on British ships. The ships sailing with letters of marque were called privateers. As more and more privateers were captured, the British found a new solution. Derelict ships were anchored in the Wallabout Bay on the East river in New York and thousands of men were sent to prison there until the war ended.

There were only 4,435 Americans who are known to have died fighting the war, but about 11,000 to 13,000 men and women died of starvation and disease aboard these ships. Naval Commissioner David Sprout and Commissioner Loring were in charge of providing for the prisoners on the ships—but like Cunningham, pocketed the money, providing the allotment for four men to be divided between six. The rations were not only meager, but of the poorest quality.

Although all the prison ships were terrible, the worst was called the *Jersey*. It housed about one thousand prisoners at a time, but between cold, starvation, and disease, an estimated 85 percent onboard died.

Even though the treatment of the Americans was terrible, treatment of foreign prisoners, mostly Spanish, was even worse. Housed in the deepest holds and fed even worse food, few of them survived.

The prison ship *Jersey* sat among the rotting hulks of other ships anchored off the New York and New Jersey coast.

This 1855 engraving shows what it may have looked like belowdecks of the *Jersey*.

George Washington knew of the mistreatment of the prisoners and wrote a letter to General Howe in protest, but conditions did not improve.

The bones of the carelessly buried dead washed up for years. Twenty years after the war, the bones were gathered up and buried in a small wooden building near the shore. In 1880, a small monument was erected. In 1908, the bones were re-interred and a new monument was erected at Fort Greene Park in Brooklyn.

The Giant Chain

The chain across the Hudson mentioned by the storekeeper really existed. The patriots had tried several times to place chains across the river, but the British had captured them. In 1777, however, Peter Townsend, under the orders of George Washington, managed to secure a huge chain five hundred yards across the Hudson River at West Point. Each link weighed about 125 pounds and the whole chain weighed more than 186 tons. It was floated and secured in place with a system of heavy rafts. The British never got a ship past this barrier.

Smallpox

Smallpox was a terrible disease that killed many people, especially the young, and often left survivors with horrible scars. The practice of variolation (deliberately infecting a person with scrapings from someone recovering from smallpox) sometimes worked, but often did not. However, it was practiced throughout most of the eighteenth century until Edward Jenner made a discovery.

Shortly after Edward Jenner developed the smallpox vaccine, this political cartoon made fun of the fact that the vaccine was developed from cowpox. The drawing shows people who have been treated by Jenner (center with white hair) with cows coming out of different parts of their bodies. Because of Jenner's vaccine, however, smallpox has been eradicated from Earth.

Jenner, who had gone through the variolation process himself, treated a milkmaid who had a disease called cowpox. For a long time, some people believed a person who had had cowpox could not get smallpox, but the theory had never been tested. Jenner tested this theory by taking scrapings from a person with cowpox and infecting his gardener's eight-year-old son. The boy got cowpox (a mild disease), but several weeks later, when he was exposed to smallpox, he was immune. It was not until 1796 that Jenner invented the smallpox vaccination (different from variolation). Until recently, children were vaccinated for smallpox. It is now considered eradicated from the earth.

The Delivery Woman

In addition to William Cunningham who appears in the story, the old woman who sold food to the prisoners was a real person in history. A few families were able to bribe guards to deliver small packages and money. For some reason, the guards tolerated the old woman. She made regular visits to the ships until she caught a fever and died. Her name has been lost to history.

Further Reading

Fiction

Dowswell, Paul. *Powder Monkey: Adventures of a Young Sailor*. New York: Bloomsbury Pub., 2005.

Maxwell, Ruth H. *Eighteen Roses Red: A Young Girl's Heroic Mission in the Revolutionary War*. Shippensburg, Pa.: White Mane Kids, 2006.

Nonfiction

Weatherly, Myra. *Women of the Sea: Ten Pirate Stories*. Greensboro, N.C.: Morgan Reynolds Pub., 2006.

Yolen, Jane. *Sea Queens: Women Pirates Around the World*. Watertown, Mass.: Charlesbridge, 2008.

Internet Addresses

The Fort Greene Park Conservancy—"The Prison Ship Martyrs Monument"
<http://www.fortgreenepark.org/pages/prisonship.htm>

Privateers and Mariners in the Revolutionary War
<http://www.usmm.org/revolution.html>

Stories From the Revolution: Privateers in the American Revolution
<http://www.nps.gov/revwar/about_the_revolution/privateers.html>